B'Elanna couldn't keep the ship together anymore. But she could still taste the victory. She wasn't about to let that go.

The ship was jolted over and over by at least a dozen disruptor blasts.

"Damage report!" Chakotay called out.

"Shields at sixty percent," Tuvok reported.

Two lights went red. B'Elanna quickly had to reroute the fuel to injectors 3 and 4. "A fuel line has ruptured. Attempting to compensate." She opened the injectors to full, but they dropped to half-impulse power. "Dammit! We're barely maintaining impulse. I can't get any more out of it."

Chakotay was flying the raider more with the manual controls than by computer. "Be creative," he said shortly.

Her eyes flashed. "How am I supposed to be 'creative' with a thirty-nine-year-old rebuilt engine!"

A bright orange flare erupted from the forward console. B'Elanna had to shield her eyes.

When her vision cleared, the Cardassian warship was looming over them, disruptor fire slashing out. Chakotay twisted and turned, managing to evade some of the blasts, but too many were landing on target.

B'Elanna saw the override in their communications, just as Gul Evek appeared on their screen. *"Maquis ship, this is Gul Evek of the Cardassian Fourth Order. Cut your engines and prepare to surrender."*

For orders other than by individual consumers, Pocket Books grants a discount on the purchase of **10 or more** copies of single titles for special markets or premium use. For further details, please write to the Vice President of Special Markets, Pocket Books, 1230 Avenue of the Americas, 9th Floor, New York, NY 10020-1586.

For information on how individual consumers can place orders, please write to Mail Order Department, Simon & Schuster Inc., 100 Front Street, Riverside, NJ 08075.

STAR TREK®

The BADLANDS

BOOK TWO OF TWO

SUSAN WRIGHT

POCKET BOOKS

New York   London   Toronto   Sydney   Singapore

This book is a work of fiction. Names, characters, places and incidents are products of the author's imagination or are used fictitiously. Any resemblance to actual events or locales or persons, living or dead, is entirely coincidental.

An *Original* Publication of POCKET BOOKS

POCKET BOOKS, a division of Simon & Schuster Inc.
1230 Avenue of the Americas, New York, NY 10020

STAR TREK is a Registered Trademark of Paramount Pictures.

A VIACOM COMPANY

This book is published by Pocket Books, a division of Simon & Schuster Inc., under exclusive license from Paramount Pictures.

ISBN: 0-671-03958-X

First Pocket Books printing December 1999

10 9 8 7 6 5 4 3 2 1

POCKET and colophon are registered trademarks of Simon & Schuster Inc.

Printed in the U.S.A.

PART 3

Stardate 48305.8
Year 2371
Prior to "Caretaker, Parts I and II"

Chapter One

CHAKOTAY STOOD at the railing overlooking the hangar bay. The *Selva*, the old raider that he commanded for the Maquis, was directly below him. Its scarred and battered hull was as familiar as an old friend. The large patch on the right warp nacelle came from one of his first battles with the Cardassians. By now he knew a lot more about evading their patrols. Plasma discharges received while traveling through the Badlands had caused the scoring along the leading edges of the bow.

Chakotay glanced up through the large oval of the hangar door above him. The forcefield tinted the view blue, much darker than the thin atmosphere of the planetoid. Beyond it, he could see the twinkling of spinning asteroids in the surrounding Terikof Belt. A dark oblong asteroid was tumbling end-over-end, skimming close to the planetoid where the Maquis base was buried.

The base was deep inside an ancient volcanic caldron, on a planetoid that would not have been able to sustain life on its surface. The Maquis had appropriated several of the abandoned mining complexes left behind by the Cardassians after the quality ore had been extracted. Since the Terikof Belt was just beyond the Moriya system, on the edge of the Badlands, plasma storms sometimes swept over the entire area. After battling the storms for generations, the Cardassians had finally abandoned their mining claims here when they also abandoned their claim to the Bajor sector.

Chakotay's hands clenched tightly around the railing as a low rumbling and shuddering shook the complex. Everyone in the bay paused for a moment and looked up, but the impact had occurred on the other side of the planetoid. They went back to work, ignoring the new layer of dust motes shaken loose into the air.

In order to live in the Terikof Belt, the Maquis had stolen a computer core capable of plotting the orbit of every piece of asteroid big enough to damage the force-field protecting the base. Right now, technicians would be calculating the effect of the impact on the trajectory of their planetoid and inputting the new data to discover if they were in danger from other asteroids.

Chakotay had participated in two evacuations since he had arrived at the base. But the Maquis had little choice in where they hid. The Terikof Belt offered safety because it was nearly impossible for the Cardassians to search all of the planetoids after their data on the asteroid movements had lapsed. The sensor shadow and plasma storms that occasionally swept over the area also managed to thoroughly confuse enemy sensors.

"Hey," Seska said, joining him at the railing. "There's a lot of activity going on. Are we pulling out again?"

Chakotay smiled at her. In the past eight months, Seska had become one of his most valued crewmembers.

"Yes, in the morning. I want you to round up the crew and make sure the *Selva* is ready to go by 0900."

"Sure." There was a leap of interest in her eyes. "How many days of supplies do we need?"

"Four days," Chakotay told her. "We'll be returning here after the mission is completed."

"Four days . . . ," she murmured speculatively. "Are we going into Cardassian territory?"

Chakotay hesitated; orders were given only to the commanders of each vessel, to be relayed to the crew on a "need-to-know" basis. But Seska was not just his right hand. They had become much closer in the past few months—and it was more than just a physical relationship. Chakotay felt that he had someone to talk to for the first time since he had suffered his crisis of faith in Starfleet and had left to join the Maquis to fight for his homeworld.

Yet Seska still maintained a distinct distance between them, making it clear that she didn't depend on him. Chakotay had hesitated to enter a relationship with *anyone,* after he realized how much he had repeatedly hurt his father and family. First he had joined

Starfleet over their objections, then the Federation had seized their homeworld and handed it over to the Cardassians as a bargaining chip for "peace." After his father had died and Chakotay had committed himself to helping his people, he didn't want to risk the possibility of letting anyone down again.

But Seska didn't ask for anything except for some light-hearted fun at the end of a long mission. She had fought the Cardassians all her life as a Bajoran terrorist, and she had joined the Maquis after peace was declared between Bajor and Cardassia.

He slipped his arm around her waist, liking the way her Bajoran nose crinkled between her eyes. "This is a big one," he told her, his voice lowering. "Eight of our ships will attack the Montee Fass shipyards in the Oliv system."

Seska's eyes widened. "That's a suicide run!"

"Not at all," Chakotay assured her. "We have intelligence indicating that their defense patrol has been shifted to the control of the Obsidian Order. There's a lot of activity in the Orias system, and we think they're priming for a strike against the Federation colonies along the border. They've left the shipyards and dozens of vessels vulnerable."

Seska slowly shook her head, as if trying to absorb the information. "Destroying Montee Fass would be a huge victory for the Maquis."

Chakotay nodded seriously. "I don't have to tell you not to say a word. I'm off to a strategic meeting to plan our attack patterns. You have a lot of work to do readying the *Selva*."

6

"Do we get some of the photon torpedoes?" she asked eagerly.

Chakotay knew that all of the Maquis had been wanting to get hold of the dozens of photon torpedoes smuggled to them by the new security chief of DS9. Very few Maquis knew that Michael Eddington was their benefactor. "You can requisition six torpedoes."

Seska whistled though her teeth. "This *is* big."

Chakotay laughed at her enthusiasm. "I'll be back at my quarters at 1100."

Seska rubbed her nose lightly against his. "Our last chance for a few days. That's my only complaint about the *Selva*—no privacy."

Chakotay gave her waist a squeeze and let go. He was smiling as he made his way down to the tactical room. He was lucky to have Seska in his life, or he would still be as dour as many of the colonists huddled in the rough, tiny rooms carved off the mining tunnels.

As he went through the tunnels to the strategic meeting, the lights were low. They flickered occasionally, because the colonists needed to conserve power consumption to elude enemy sensors. Children were playing on the dirty floors, since they had no place else to go, no sunshine on their faces, no wind to freshen the air.

Chakotay hurried faster, knowing their future depended on him and the other Maquis fighters.

Seska went straight down to the hangar bay to gather the twenty-member crew. They had to begin preparing the raider for departure. She assigned duties to everyone, firmly clutching her Bajoran persona around herself. She was constantly aware of the time, knowing there was something critical she needed to do. But she tried not to think about it, because she couldn't risk letting her mask slip now.

When everything seemed to be under control, with B'Elanna giving the engines one last diagnostic and Ricci superintending the loading of the photon torpedoes, Seska finally slipped away. Even as she walked through the corridors, she refused to allow herself to think of the implications of this raid on Montee Fass.

She took the precaution of locking the door to her quarters, which she shared with B'Elanna whenever they were at the base. Crawling under her bunk, she reached for the panel she could pop open with her stylus. Concealed underneath was the headset transmitter unit she used to communicate with her Cardassian contact, Gul Evek.

Seska had undergone surgery to transform her Cardassian features into those of a Bajoran two years ago. First she had been sent to Earth to stake out Starfleet Academy and gather intelligence. When she made contact with a Starfleet defector who was joining the Maquis, she had been ordered to join the Maquis as well. It had been a long and grueling assignment. But now it looked like all of her work was about to pay off.

She placed the silver bands over her head, with the visor projecting a handsbreadth away from her face. The transmitter sent out a quantum carrier wave, which could transport a limited amount of information for a short distance. There was only a narrow window of time in which she could send a message Gul Evek could pick up on the *Vetar*. The *Galor*-class warship cruised through the nearby Moriya system on a regular schedule.

The low bandwidth resulted in a tiny image of Gul Evek's face, flattened and gray-toned. Seska knew her own face appeared on his viewscreen similarly distorted.

"I have something," Seska reported.

"It better be the location of a Maquis base," Gul Evek demanded.

"Negative," Seska reported. Only the Maquis commanders knew the coordinates of their home base. If the commander was killed on a mission, their ship was forced to rendezvous with another Maquis vessel in order for the new commander to obtain the coordinates. After nearly a year of observing the Maquis, Seska had concluded that the Maquis who had defected from Starfleet and brought with them Starfleet knowledge and protocols, had produced a truly formidable terrorist group.

Gul Evek's mature face twisted in disgust. "You have accomplished nothing—"

"Do you want my report or not?" Seska shot back. "I could always explain to Central Command that you ignored my data."

She didn't want to anger Gul Evek too much, but she needed him to treat this seriously. It had taken a long time, but now she had the information they'd been waiting for. *Now* they could strike a decisive blow against the Maquis. Those attack ships would have full crew compliments and eight Maquis commanders.

Surely someone would break under interrogation and reveal the location of the bases in the Badlands sector.

"Proceed," Evek ordered, as if she were trying his patience.

"At least eight Maquis ships will depart the Terikof Belt tomorrow morning at 0900," she reported. "The target is the Montee Fass shipyards in the Oliv system."

Gul Evek's surprise was almost worth every day she had spent in this mining hole.

"Are you certain?" he demanded. "Who is your source?"

"Chakotay, the commander of the *Selva* himself. We are preparing to depart now." Seska wasn't going to explain the degree to which she had been forced to become intimate with Chakotay before he would share any sensitive information with her.

"Excellent," Gul Evek said. Seska got the feeling he was talking to himself, not her. "We will lay a trap for the Maquis. . . ."

"And you can pull me out," Seska reminded him.

He considered her for a long moment. "Yes, it is time for a complete debriefing. You can always reinfiltrate, if need be."

"Yes," she agreed evenly, suppressing a shudder. She had hoped to get a nice promotion out of this assignment. She was ready to supervise or train new agents, instead of risking her life every day in the field. Nearly ten years of successful undercover assignments was plenty for any agent.

"In fact," Gul Evek continued. "There's something

else you can do before you leave. There is a Starfleet spy among the Maquis."

"A spy?" she asked, startled. "You were withholding information from me?"

"It was not necessary to reveal the identity of the individual to you." Gul Evek's voice hardened. "Now it is. You will plant evidence that will implicate this spy in betraying the planned raid on Montee Fass. It will appear that Starfleet alerted Central Command and allowed us to ambush the Maquis."

Seska had to smile. "Nice. Who is it?"

"A Vulcan called Tuvok."

"Tuvok . . ." Seska didn't doubt for an instant that Gul Evek was right.

When Tuvok had arrived a month ago, the Vulcan had claimed that his wife and children had been killed by Cardassians during a raid on a nearby Federation colony. But he was a typical Vulcan, too dispassionate and too decorous to fit in easily with the rebels and mercenaries who fought for the Maquis.

For some reason, Chakotay had trusted Tuvok from the first moment they found him in an escape pod that was almost out of air. Then again that didn't say much, because Chakotay trusted her, too.

"I'll leave something here that will implicate him," Seska assured Gul Evek. "When we don't return, our personal items will be searched."

"Tuvok reports to a Captain Janeway," Gul Evek added. "The Maquis should be able to confirm that he is her chief of security, still on active duty in Starfleet."

Seska made some notes. "The registry of my raider

is 078-Gamma-A-905, the *Selva*. Please don't blow us up while you're taking care of the others."

Gul Evek smiled as if that thought had never occurred to him. His middle-aged face suddenly looked young again, like the warrior of legend. "This mission will bring great glory to Cardassia."

"For the honor of Cardassia," Seska agreed, before signing off.

She sighed and leaned back against the bulkhead. It was good to know Evek was on her side. Sometimes during the long months when she had had little to give him, she knew he had considered writing her off as a source. But even Gul Evek received his orders from higher up, and would have had to answer to the Obsidian Order for anything that happened to her.

And finally, this information was better than anything she had hoped for. All those nights spent with that human male were paying off at last.

Quickly, she created a text message that appeared to have been sent from Captain Janeway, briefly confirming the receipt of Tuvok's information that a Maquis attack fleet was planning to strike the Montee Fass shipyards. She ran it through her transmitter to imprint the code with the stardate. This would make it appear that Tuvok betrayed the Maquis to Janeway shortly after the information had been given to the commanders.

Pulling on her gloves, she transferred the text message to a disc that came from a sealed container. It was untraceable to either her or Cardassia, having been purchased from a Ferengi over a year ago. As long as she didn't touch it, none of her DNA would contaminate the magnetic surfaces.

Then she quickly dismantled the transmitter headset and stowed the pieces in the bottom of her bag. She couldn't leave anything behind that would implicate her as a spy. She might be able to make use of these contacts in the future. After all, many a brilliant career had been built in a war.

Seska slung her bag over one shoulder and gave the room one last look.

The tunnels were bustling. Even if Chakotay hadn't told her that a big raid was in the works, she would have known something was going on from the atmosphere on the base. Everyone was tense, excited, hopeful. She wondered what it would be like when the eight ships didn't return. What would happen when their finest base was discovered? It could rip the guts out of the Maquis. Thanks to her.

Tuvok was staying in a small room two levels down in the old mining quarters. She ran down the darkened spiral staircase that curved though the borehole, hoping Tuvok wasn't there.

She knocked again and again, but there was no answer. The door was locked, which was unusual on the Maquis base. Everyone had lost so much that there was nothing left worth stealing. The crew tended to keep most of their belongings on the ship so they could leave at an instant's notice.

Seska didn't have time for subtlety. She glanced around to be sure no one could see her in the alcove of the door, then she jammed the Cardassian stylus into the groove of the door. With a twist, it released a burst of ferroplasmic energy. The action depleted the last of the reserves in the stylus, but the door popped open.

She kissed the stylus and tucked it into her brown leather jacket. It had been a most useful tool.

Inside, the room was dark, but her eyes retained the Cardassian ability to see in dim light. She quickly slipped the disc into the space behind the desk. Tuvok wouldn't notice it, but a routine scan would pick up the magnetic traces. It would appear to have fallen unnoticed.

The door slid open, letting in more light. "What are you doing in my quarters?" Tuvok asked behind her.

"Tuvok! I was looking for you. You didn't report to the ship," she said accusingly.

"I did. I have just returned for my belongings," Tuvok told her.

"Good," she said briskly, folding her arms. "Get them and let's go. I need help with that lateral sensor grid. The energy conduits still seem to be congested."

Tuvok pulled clothing from his drawers and packed his bag. "I have attempted to reroute the conduits, Seska, but the ship is quite old."

"I know, but I've got another idea." Seska bounced on her toes, the perfect image of a rebel wanting to get to their ship.

Tuvok gathered up the photographs of his wife and children. He looked at them a moment, and Seska could almost believe they were his wife and children. Not dead, though. She was almost positive that was just his cover story.

The thought emboldened her. Tuvok was the spy—
he was the one who should be worried.

"Come on," she insisted, starting to sound suspicious. "If I didn't know you better, I would think you're stalling."

"Not at all." Tuvok glanced at the door on the way out, but the ferroplasma had left no visible traces. He undoubtedly didn't want to ask how she had gotten into his locked room, since locked rooms were so unusual in the Maquis base.

Seska smiled as his back turned. She didn't need to glance at the desk to know the disc was still there, waiting to be discovered after the ambush. Quite neatly done, she congratulated herself.

Now she had to finish the preparations for the *Selva's* departure tomorrow. And unfortunately she would have to continue her ruse with Chakotay. Just the thought of it made her ache for this assignment to end.

Chapter Two

THE RAIDER swung around the Badlands, staying deep within the sensor shadow that stretched 10 million kilometers around the plasma storms. When they finally reached open space, B'Elanna felt a rush of pure joy. She lived for moments like these.

The Maquis war was custom-made for her. Her Klingon mother was probably still on Kronos, though B'Elanna didn't have contact with her anymore. And she hadn't talked to her human father since she was a little girl. She was missed by nobody, and had no other place to go.

"Setting course for the Oliv system," Chakotay announced. "Warp 4."

"Warp 4," B'Elanna confirmed, carefully watching the antimatter reaction gauge.

Warp 4 was the best speed that several of their vessels could make. It was a motley assortment of ships, but she was convinced that together they formed a formidable battle fleet. The *Selva* was capable of higher speeds and had plenty of power for weapons. B'Elanna was ready for a fight.

She sat behind Chakotay, who was piloting the raider in the bow seat. Seska climbed through the round hatch and flicked B'Elanna a victory signal before sitting down at the other monitor. Tuvok was at the side station, keeping watch on sensors for Cardassian warships. Ever since they had left the shadow of the Badlands, their fleet was vulnerable.

"You've done a good job with her, B'Elanna," Chakotay said. "I can feel the difference in the reaction timing. Much more responsive under warp."

"We could go as high as Warp 6," she told him proudly, ignoring the praise.

"Nice to know we have it if we need it," Chakotay said.

B'Elanna appreciated Chakotay's support. They had become friends over the past few months. She had never been good at making friends, neither on the human colony world where she had been born nor on the Klingon homeworld where her mother had taken her after divorcing her father. B'Elanna had found out the hard way how difficult it was to survive without a family name or friends.

B'Elanna had once thought Starfleet offered a way out of that dirt-scrubbing misery, but she had been wrong. Starfleet was rigid and only wanted round pegs for their round holes. They had no need for individuals who thought things could be done better without following Starfleet protocols.

That's why she was out here, doing a job Starfleet should have done, destroying a shipyard of warships to keep the Cardassians from attacking Federation colonies. She hoped Starfleet would wake up some day and start fighting the real battle instead of trying to capture Maquis fighters. Perhaps their raid on the shipyards would spark new support for the Maquis in the Federation.

She glanced up at the viewscreen, at the magnified image of other starships in their convoy traveling in front of them. To avoid sending out a strong energy signal, they maintained a loose formation, with nearly one million kilometers between the *Selva* and the lead ship. The gleaming silver and black hulls were a satisfying sight.

Suddenly the nose of the lead ship tilted sharply upward. With the instincts of a born engineer, B'Elanna recognized a subspace shockwave when she saw one.

"Red Alert!" she cried out, initiating the shutdown sequence, instantly dropping the *Selva* out of warp.

Chakotay was turning to her questioningly when the shock wave hit the raider.

Luckily B'Elanna was belted into her seat, as were the other crew members. The power failure and gravity generator overload made her strain against the restraints. Several monitors were beeping to signal power failure.

B'Elanna was busy assisting the emergency shutdown of the major systems when the emergency power finally kicked in and gravity came back online. She was glad that weightlessness didn't make her sick to her stomach. Seska looked practically green.

"What was that!" Chakotay demanded through the beeping.

"Sensors are off-line," Tuvok announced. "We encountered a subspace shockwave consisting of tetryon neutrinos."

"The Badlands curse?" Chakotay asked. "This far away from the plasma storms?"

"Apparently so," Tuvok confirmed.

B'Elanna had heard about the Badlands curse from fellow Maquis. One woman had described how the subspace shockwave had practically torn their ship apart when it hit them traveling at Warp 5.

"Warp drive is off-line," B'Elanna finally reported, once she was certain that antimatter containment was holding and the power was bleeding off in a bloom of plasma. She had managed to drop the warp field just in time to save the warp core.

"How long until you can get warp drive back online?" Chakotay asked.

B'Elanna shook her head. "Several of the EPS circuits have to be replaced. That could take an hour."

"What about impulse power?" he asked.

"We should have that any time," she assured him. "And weapons systems don't seem to be affected."

She was sure the other ships weren't so lucky. The *Selva* shook slightly, as if from a repercussion wave.

"Somebody had a warp-core breach," B'Elanna said as the others looked up. "We still have shields—"

The *Selva* shook again from another explosion.

"Sensors?" Chakotay asked.

"We have partial sensors," Tuvok confirmed. "Range 100,000 kilometers. The *Defender* has suffered a warp-core breach, but the core had been ejected. I am unable to lock onto the entire fleet. . . ."

"A hundred thousand kilometers—that's firing range!" B'Elanna protested. "We'll be lucky to see a patrol before they blow us away."

"I am attempting to boost sensors," Tuvok calmly replied. "There is an incoming message from Commander Maus."

Chakotay turned to the small screen high up in the bulkhead as the commander of the flagship appeared. "Status, Chakotay?"

"We'll have warp drive up in an hour or so. Sensor range is 100,000 kilometers," he tersely reported.

"Structural damage?" Commander Maus asked.

"B'Elanna?" Chakotay prompted.

"None, sir. We dropped out of warp just in time."

The commander sighed. "You're in better shape than the rest of us. Some ships are still on emergency power and have no impulse capability. They'll have to be towed. Two vessels ejected their warp cores."

Chakotay's hand formed a fist to rest on the console. "We have to retreat."

"Yes, I've ordered the others to withdraw, Alpha pattern."

"We can take up the perimeter," Chakotay offered.

"Good." The commander gave him a grim nod. "See you at the base."

The screen went dark as B'Elanna cried in outrage, "No!"

Chakotay shot her a look that silenced her. "What do you want us to do? *Crawl* into Cardassian territory? It would take weeks to reach the Oliv system on impulse."

"I'll get you warp power," B'Elanna protested.

"But we're only one ship," Chakotay pointed out.

Tuvok agreed, "Our only reasonable option is to retreat."

"You *would* say that!" Seska snapped at the Vulcan. "We can't just run away."

B'Elanna felt a surge of hope when Seska agreed with her.

Usually Chakotay agreed with Seska, but this time his expression was forbidding. "We follow our orders." He turned back to the helm. "Laying in the Alpha pattern retreat."

The viewscreen showed the Badlands as a ruddy fist-sized blotch in the distance. The droning beeps had ceased, and the computer consoles had returned to their normal whirs and flashing indicator lights. All was calm on the bridge again.

B'Elanna wanted to scream. She knew it was madness to strike into Cardassian territory with only one ship, but she still wanted to try.

She abruptly released her belt and stood up. "I've got to check the power grid."

Chakotay didn't glance back as he dismissed her.

He probably knew she was lying. B'Elanna didn't
meet anyone's eyes as she climbed down the ladder,
brushing past the other crew members without saying
a word. They started to ask questions about removing
the primary EPS taps to the warp drive, but they
abruptly shut their mouths at the sight of her face.
She passed deep into the engine room of the tiny
ship.

Standing between the thrumming impulse generators, B'Elanna threw back her head and screamed in
absolute fury.

Tuvok noted that as soon as B'Elanna left the bridge
Seska turned to Chakotay and said, "I think you're
making a BIG mistake."

Chakotay was busy programming the navigator and
plotting their return course. "It's not your decision,
Seska." He sounded aggravated.

"This is our only chance to get Montee Fass!"

"If you have a suggestion about repairing seven
warp drives on the run, I'd like to hear it. Otherwise, let
me do my job."

There was a warning tone in Chakotay's voice,
which ended Seska's open objections for the moment,
though she continued to mutter about all their effort
gone to waste. There was a bitter tang of defeat in the
air, remnants of human sweat and adrenaline. Yet
Tuvok ascertained that Seska was particularly distressed about the cancellation of their mission; he was
at a loss to explain why.

Tuvok often felt as if there was more going on than

he could perceive. He carefully noted every nuance of each individual's action and words, knowing that the information analysts at Starfleet Headquarters would have a much larger context in which to place his data. It was not necessary for him to draw conclusions, only to report what occurred.

Nevertheless, Tuvok had gained quite a comprehensive picture of the capability and morale of the Maquis. The rebel forces were kept remarkably well supplied by unnamed sources, were adequately staffed, and were gaining strategic ground.

Lieutenant Thomas Riker had recently infused the Maquis with confidence after he had hijacked the *Defiant* and helped them launch a preemptive strike against Cardassian forces. Even when Captain Sisko of DS9 had joined with the Cardassians to capture the renegade Lieutenant, the Maquis had simply turned Riker into a martyr for their cause when he was sentenced to life imprisonment in the Lazon II labor camp. Defections from Starfleet were increasing, and Tuvok was beginning to wonder if he would encounter someone he knew before his mission came to an end.

Tuvok had three weeks remaining on his current mission. Then he would take up his new duties as chief of security on board *Voyager,* the new starship being completed at Utopia Planetia. The ship had been uniquely outfitted for deep space scientific missions, and was equipped to enter plasma storms. After his covert reconnaissance mission, Tuvok was certain they would use *Voyager* to explore the Badlands thoroughly and search for several Maquis bases rumored to be on planets inside the plasma storms.

It was Tuvok's expert opinion that the Maquis were a threat to both Cardassia and the Federation. They were destabilizing the area during a time when the Federation needed to concentrate on the danger posed by the Dominion, who had access to the Alpha Quadrant through the nearby Bajoran wormhole.

Tuvok was particularly interested in the outcome of their present mission, because it centered on the fact that the Obsidian Order had commandeered over a dozen of the best ships in their fleet. Tuvok did not agree with the Maquis that the Cardassian Empire would strike Federation colonies. That simply showed the narrow territorial view held by the Maquis, who did not think in galactic terms. Tuvok believed the Cardassians were massing for an attack on the Dominion, and was curious as to how they would go about it.

He was pleased that he would now be able to inform Captain Janeway that the attack on Montee Fass had been canceled. If the Maquis had been successful, it could have done serious damage to the Cardassian capability to wage their search and destroy campaigns against the rebels. It also could have resulted in additional pressure from Cardassia's Central Command for assistance from Starfleet.

He considered it ironic that their convoy was defeated by the same phenomenon that had disrupted the systems on board the *Enterprise-D* just a few years ago. Because of that incident, the brief Federation truce with

Cardassia had almost been broken. This time, the damage caused by the phenomenon had prevented Cardassian bloodshed.

Once power to the sensors was restored, Tuvok continually monitored the *Selva*'s trajectory and the surrounding area. The *Selva* swung wide toward the Cardassian border, where warships would most likely appear if their convoy was detected. They had full impulse power with warp on the way, while six of the other Maquis ships were severely disabled, proceeding at half-impulse speed directly toward the Badlands. Tuvok estimated it would take the convoy eight hours to reach the safety of the Badlands sensor shadow.

"Any sign of activity along the Cardassian border?" Chakotay asked.

"None, sir." The honorific slipped out, a trained instinct after decades of Starfleet duty.

B'Elanna was just returning to the bridge. "No patrols?" she repeated incredulously. "We're limping along out here, and the Cardassians haven't even noticed?"

Tuvok refrained from replying. He was growing accustomed to the engineer's aggressive speech patterns.

Her irritability did not appear to disturb Chakotay. "Sensor range?" Chakotay requested.

"On screen." Tuvok posted the map of the sensor data on the small viewscreen over Chakotay's head so everyone could see it. "Long-range sensors encompass an area that extends into Cardassian territory."

"That's the Opek Nor space station," Chakotay commented, pointing to the nearest base inside sensor range. "There are usually patrols nearby."

"The planetary defenses are activated," Tuvok confirmed. "However, there are no vessels in the region."

B'Elanna stood at Tuvok's shoulder, craning for a better look. "They've gone someplace else. Could the patrols be near the Badlands, waiting to ambush the convoy?"

"Unlikely," Tuvok said firmly. "If Opek Nor had detected our convoy, they would have engaged us while we were heading into Cardassian territory."

"Then Opek Nor is undefended," B'Elanna said speculatively.

Seska snorted. "Are you kidding? That station is protected by the best planetary defense lasers you can find."

"So it appears," Chakotay agreed, examining the navigational data. "But I know a thing or two about Opek Nor. At warp 6, we could get there in two hours, make a decisive strike, and be back at the Badlands not long after the convoy gets there."

"Are you crazy?" Seska demanded. "First you cancel our mission, and now you want to attack a new target without any reconnaissance?"

"Our target is whatever we can find," B'Elanna retorted happily.

Chakotay opened a channel to Commander Maus, who was in charge of their convoy. Tuvok knew she was a former Starfleet captain, well aware of the advantages to be gained if something could be salvaged from their mission. The Opek Nor space station was a serious impediment to the Maquis because they supplied and maintained the patrols that swept through the Badlands sector. Tuvok was uncertain why the Cardassians had left the station undefended.

After reviewing the sensor data, Commander Maus agreed to allow Chakotay to take their raider into Cardassian territory and strike Opek Nor. Maus ordered, "Target for structural damage as we discussed. Good luck, Chakotay."

"You can count on us. Chakotay out." He was grinning at the news, and B'Elanna let out a little hurrah as she returned to her seat.

"We can't risk it!" Seska blurted out. "The patrols are probably hiding on the other side of the planet or doing exercises. Or our sensors are too damaged to detect them."

"We'll find out soon enough," Chakotay told her. "Setting course for Opek Nor. Warp 6."

"Warp 6," B'Elanna confirmed.

Chakotay opened a channel to the rest of the ship. "Crew, we have a new mission. The Opek Nor space station is currently undefended. Since we're nearby, we might as well pay them a visit. Prepare for battle stations."

From the muted sound of cheers, Tuvok could tell the crew was pleased by their new orders. It confirmed his suspicions—that the Maquis were gaining momentum, despite their setbacks.

"Let's get her," Chakotay said cheerfully.

Seska slammed her hands down on the console. "This is insane!"

The note of hysteria made everyone look at her. Chakotay's voice was mild, as he asked, "Is something wrong, Seska?"

She seemed confused for a moment, shaking her head, realizing she was overreacting.

Tuvok took his tricorder from his pocket and turned. "May I scan you?"

"What for?" she demanded defensively.

"In prior encounters with the Badlands," Tuvok explained. "It was noted that tetryon radiation sickness affected random members of the crew."

Seska put a hand to her head. "I am feeling a little sick. I have to go lie down."

Before Tuvok could scan her, she got up and stumbled to the hatch.

"Are you okay?" B'Elanna called out, concerned. "Do you need any help?"

"I'm fine," Seska replied shortly, disappearing.

"Let her go," Chakotay said, his forehead furrowed in concern.

Tuvok asked B'Elanna, "May I?" When she nodded, he scanned both her and Chakotay, then himself and the crew members at the rear of the bridge. "Maximum exposure, 100 rads each. That is not serious. However, other members of the crew may have received higher doses."

Chakotay paused, obviously considering the danger of that uncertainty and wondering if they should continue to Opek Nor. "We'll stay on course and see what happens to the rest of the crew in the next couple of hours."

* * *

Seska was cursing as she climbed down to the room she shared with three other crewmembers. Of all the terrible luck in the galaxy! It was bad enough that their mission had been aborted, but this new plan to attack Opek Nor could be disastrous.

She dug through her bag and pulled out the silver bands of the quantum transmitter. Gul Evek's starship was quite likely out of range of the carrier wave, preparing to assist the main battle force with their ambush of the Maquis in the Oliv system. She would have to send an emergency-burst transmission and hope Evek picked it up before the *Selva* reached Opek Nor.

Unfortunately, there was no way she could warn the station itself. She wasn't worried that the station couldn't protect itself. She was more afraid she would be destroyed along with everyone else on the *Selva* during their futile attack.

She slid to the foot of her bunk where the half-cover would hide her from view. Quickly she assembled the device and entered the sequence to activate the emergency signal.

Jamming it over her head, she took a few deep breaths. She could send at most a ten-second message along with the preprogrammed emergency-burst transmission. She would have to hope that Tuvok had devoted all of their power to scanning the system for Cardassian patrols and would not detect her internal communication. At this point, even if he did, she felt she had little to lose.

"The Maquis convoy has aborted the attack on Montee Fass," she whispered urgently. "They were damaged in an encounter with the Badlands curse. They will attack Opek Nor, repeat, attack underway on Opek Nor—"

The signal beeped that she had recorded the maximum amount of information. Seska considered re-recording the burst, knowing how frantic she sounded. But it would take some time to reach Gul Evek and she couldn't waste a single moment.

Seska initiated the transmission.

As she disassembled the transmitter, she shook her head ruefully. She could almost see the Cardassian battle plan like a textbook case. They had withdrawn the patrols from this section of the Cardassian border, anticipating the incursion to occur a light-year away. All of these preparations had been done according to the information she had supplied. The failure would rest on her shoulders.

She could only hope that Gul Evek received the message in time to stop the Maquis from striking Opek Nor. He was sure to let nothing stop him. After all, it was in his best interest, too. As her contact, he would already carry much responsibility for the failure of the Montee Fass strike to occur.

Seska gathered the silver bands into a bundle and tucked them in the lining of her jacket. She headed down to engineering, intending to conceal the transmitter in case her communique had been detected.

More importantly, she hoped to find a way to sabotage the *Selva* before it could reach Opek Nor. The best place to do that was on the bridge, but she was too wary of Tuvok and his tricorder. Since Tuvok was a Starfleet spy, his equipment could be technically superior to Maquis devices. She had undergone DNA grafts to deceive routine scans, but she had been warned that a thorough Starfleet medical exam could detect her true heritage.

Since the bridge was not an option, she headed down to engineering to see what she could do. It would take longer, but she was certain she could find some way to stop the raider.

Chapter Three

CHAKOTAY WAS SWEATING. One of the symptoms of mild
tetryon radiation poisoning, Tuvok had explained.
Tuvok passed the cellular regenerator over each one of
the bridge crew, assuring them that the symptoms
would pass within a few hours. Chakotay was mostly
able to ignore it.

B'Elanna didn't seem affected in the least, but she
was on a battle high and probably wouldn't have noticed a direct phaser blast. Chakotay was accustomed to
her Klingon-style rage during a fight, and usually he
found a way to turn it to their advantage. With Seska
out of commission, he was glad B'Elanna's keen edge
had not been blunted by the radiation exposure. Tuvok,
too, seemed to be holding up with typical Vulcan calm.

Aside from Seska, three other crewmembers had to
retire to their bunks—altogether one-fifth of his crew

was ill. But he had run the *Selva* with only ten people, so he did not cancel their attack on Opek Nor. It was essential that they return to the Terikof base with some sort of victory in hand.

"Dropping to full impulse power," Chakotay announced. He brought them into the Opek Nor system. He wished they could maintain warp speed, but that was impossible so close to the gravitational pull of the sun. Still, using the sun to block their approach, the *Selva* would be able to sneak up on the station.

Chakotay usually trusted Seska's opinion, because she was a skilled Bajoran terrorist, having fought Cardassians most of her adult life. But this time she didn't have all of the information.

Several months ago, Chakotay had been one of a handful of commanders who had been briefed on the stolen specs of Opek Nor and the planetary defense grid. The specs had been smuggled to the Maquis by Captain Yates, but the contact who had delivered them to Yates had disappeared shortly afterward. So the Maquis had deemed it too dangerous to attempt an attack on the station.

But the commanders had analyzed Opek Nor's vulnerable points. They had determined that if the defense patrol could be drawn away, a certain attack pattern could penetrate the planetary defenses. Photon torpedoes aimed at a particular structural weakness had a 77-percent chance of disabling the station.

The key to success was diverting the defense patrols. And according to all sensor sweeps over the past two hours, Opek Nor was currently undefended by patrols.

Susan Wright

Chakotay wasn't going to question why. At full impulse, they approached Opek Nor at one-quarter light speed.

"Passing the nimbus of the sun," Tuvok announced.

"Ready photon torpedoes," Chakotay ordered. Opek Nor had adequate shielding to deflect dozens of phaser blasts, but photon torpedoes created a deformation wave even when they didn't penetrate the shields. The Maquis simulations had shown that the deformation wave could start an adverse chain reaction in the sensitive joint that held the docking ring to the station.

The viewscreen focused on the image of Opek Nor. It was a midsized Cardassian station. A circular docking ring was joined by three spokes to a stout vertical post in the center. The top and bottom of the post had three curving ports for warships, the classic Cardassian hook design featured in everything from their space stations to their public buildings. Currently there were no ships docked anywhere on the structure.

"Forward shields on maximum," Chakotay ordered.

"Shields up," Tuvok confirmed.

"Target the joints of two spokes where they join the main vertical section," Chakotay ordered. "Two photon torpedoes in rapid succession on each spoke. That should destroy its structural integrity."

"Loss of structural integrity could cause the station to descend into the atmosphere of the planet," Tuvok noted.

"That's the plan," Chakotay confirmed.

Tuvok turned. "I am reading 342 Cardassians on board."

"They've got plenty of life pods," Chakotay said grimly.

He hoped they would have time to evacuate. As the *Selva* emerged from the sun at full impulse, Opek Nor would just be seeing their approach. If they didn't have time to evacuate . . . well, this was war. Far too many of his fellow fighters had been killed by Cardassians, both during his time in Starfleet and with the Maquis.

Chakotay carefully set their approach heading to avoid the planetary defense grid. If they kept the station between themselves and the raider, the grid couldn't fire. But he knew it would be tight—especially the turn.

The *Selva* shuddered under the rapid-fire impact of Opek Nor's disrupters. But shields held firm.

"We're making our approach," Chakotay announced. "Prepare to fire thrusters."

"Thrusters ready," B'Elanna called out. She had instantly understood the maneuver when Chakotay explained it to her.

Chakotay kept an eye on the target parameters, noting they narrowed much faster than he would have preferred. But they had to be moving fast to perform the maneuver and get back out.

The planetary defense grid fired green phasers. They created a crisscross pattern just outside the cone of space around the raider.

"Entering target range!" Tuvok announced.

"Fire!" Chakotay ordered.

"Firing photon torpedoes," Tuvok reported.

Two streaks of red sped toward the station. Then two more.

Chakotay held his breath and held course at full impulse, knowing they might have time to send another salvo. But the torpedoes hit perfectly at the joint of the spokes one after the other as the station spun in place.

"Direct hits," Tuvok announced.

"Now! Impulse engines off-line!" Chakotay called out.

B'Elanna dropped the impulse engines off-line. In that instant's pause, Chakotay hit the front port and the rear starboard thrusters full-power.

He did it by instinct, by the feel of the ship. A .33 second burst and the station had turned into a streak of silver as the raider spun neatly in place.

"Impulse power!" he ordered, as he hit both rear thrusters.

"I've lost impulse!" B'Elanna exclaimed.

Chakotay continued to engage thrusters as the raider moved away from the station. He adjusted their course to stay in a nearly direct line with their approach.

B'Elanna was working frantically to get impulse drive back on-line.

When Chakotay was sure their trajectory would keep them protected by the station, he switched the view toward the rear to watch the slowly receding station. Two of the spokes were crumpled near the central post, and one bent further, deforming the docking ring.

"The station is losing structural integrity," Tuvok announced. "The orbit is destabilizing."

Chakotay had to alter course to keep the shifting station between the *Selva* and the planetary defense grid.

Opek Nor was turning, and several-dozen life pods had suddenly blossomed from the outer ring.

"Where's that impulse drive?" he demanded.

"I don't understand it," B'Elanna exclaimed. "The accelerator went out of alignment. It doesn't make any sense—"

"I don't care how it happened!" Chakotay shuddered at the thought of the station going down while they were still in range of the planetary defense grid. They would be pulverized. "Just get me impulse power *now*."

On screen, the station had ceased spinning and was slowly tumbling end-over-end. Fragments were flying off, along with life pods, so many that Chakotay couldn't count them all.

The drag of the atmosphere finally stopped the station from tumbling. Streamers of white peeled off the leading edges, causing the central structural member to collapse in half. The ring bent then twisted as it collided with the atmosphere. For a moment, the structure held together, then it exploded into a ball of fire and debris.

"Impulse drive on-line!" B'Elanna exclaimed.

It was only one-half impulse, but it was enough. The raider shot forward as several lances pierced the place where they had just been. Several more phasers reached out, but Chakotay's evasive actions eluded them. He could tell the planetary defense system was hampered by all the life pods between the planet and the *Selva*. Lucky for them.

"Any patrol ships?" Chakotay asked Tuvok.

"Negative, sir."

Chakotay concentrated on flying until they were well out of range. As soon as the lances stopped, he hit the comm to the rest of the ship. "We did it! Opek Nor has been destroyed!"

He could hear the crew shout their approval. It would certainly improve the situation of the Maquis in the Badlands sector. They could even press their advantage and attack nearby colonies, while the Cardassian patrols would have to travel to the closest resupply port, a light-year away.

With B'Elanna actually laughing out loud and the rest of his crew still calling out their victory, Chakotay knew that despite the risk, he had done the right thing.

"Let's go home, everyone," he told them.

Tuvok was aware that he was the only one on the bridge who did not participate in the joyous reaction when Opek Nor was destroyed. He assumed his Vulcan nature would explain his placidity.

It was odd that the Cardassians had left Opek Nor undefended by patrol ships.

"Engaging warp power," Chakotay informed the bridge. "Warp four."

"What's wrong, Tuvok?" B'Elanna asked in a teasing tone. "Feeling sorry for the Cardassians?"

Chakotay laughed, but Tuvok said seriously, "It was too easy."

"You call that easy!" B'Elanna retorted. "We barely got out alive."

Chakotay lifted one hand, placating the engineer. "How long before we reach the Badlands shadow?"

Tuvok called up a schematic of the narrow border of space around the Badlands. "At our current speed, four hours twenty-seven minutes."

B'Elanna frowned. "I should be able to give you warp 6 in a few minutes."

"That would shorten the time considerably," Chakotay said speculatively.

For a while, the bridge was silent again as the crew worked to get warp drive up to full speed. Tuvok continued to scan the region meticulously for Cardassian vessels.

They were traveling at warp 6 and were not far from the Badlands sensor shadow when Tuvok picked up signs of a Cardassian warship on long-range sensors. He aimed additional sensors toward the ship and confirmed.

"Warship on long-range sensors," he announced, "Bearing eight-seven-zero mark forty. Approaching at warp 9."

"When will they intercept?" Chakotay demanded.

"In approximately eight minutes." That was close to the edge of the Badlands sensor shadow. At least the warship would have to drop out of warp, which would give them equal tactical advantage.

"Ready photon torpedoes," Chakotay ordered.

Tuvok prepared the final two torpedoes, knowing they would do little good against the heavy shields of a *Galor*-class warship.

Chakotay switched the screen on, so they could see the warship approaching. Tuvok also followed their course on his console. The blip of the warship closed in ominously fast.

"That's the *Vetar*," Chakotay said. "Our old friend Gul Evek."

From the commander's tone, Tuvok determined Chakotay had engaged this warship before with little success.

The tactical situation looked quite bad for the Maquis raider. Tuvok faced the facts without fear. He had been reluctant to accept this undercover mission; however, Starfleet had deemed it critical to determine the current situation of the Maquis. Though the risk was great, Tuvok had agreed. If he was to become the chief of security for Captain Janeway, he needed to know the dangers in this region of space.

"Dropping out of warp," Chakotay announced as they entered the sensor shadow of the Badlands.

"The warship is entering weapons range," Tuvok reported. "Approaching at full-impulse power."

"Full power to the rear shields," Chakotay ordered.

"The *Vetar* is firing weapons," Tuvok informed them.

The first phase disruptor blast bounced harmlessly off their shields. But it shook the little vessel, even from such a great distance. The lights on the bridge dimmed as more power was routed to defensive systems.

As at other times of great stress, Tuvok could pick up brief telepathic sensory bursts from each mind around him: B'Elanna's rage at the injustice of their situation, Chakotay's focused attention on the helm, even members of the crew below decks, fear at each disruptor jolt. For a moment, Tuvok sensed Seska's desperate hope and terror spiking through the others. Then it was gone.

A lifetime of training in the Kolinahr discipline enabled Tuvok to achieve a calm, centered state despite the turmoil on the raider. He was prepared for anything.

Chapter Four

SESKA COULDN'T TAKE any of the main engineering stations without drawing questions from Chakotay, so she stayed below at secondary stations, asking the others not to tell the commander. She insisted that she was well enough to assist and didn't want to be sent back to her bunk.

Because of her peripheral position, Seska had only been able to disrupt impulse power for a brief interval, by overriding the IPS command coordinator. But she was too late—the raider had already fired torpedoes at Opek Nor. As it turned out, she almost destroyed the *Selva* by putting them in danger from the planetary defense grid.

But B'Elanna was a brilliant engineer, and she had somehow bypassed the command coordinator in engineering manually and rerouted the IPS through secondary systems. After that, Seska had scrambled to find something she could sabotage without being immediately discovered. She didn't want to get killed on the spot for her efforts.

When the raider was hit by the first phase disruptor impacts, she felt a leap of joy. The raider wasn't going to escape after all. Then word flashed through the ship that it was Gul Evek attacking them, and the expressions on the crew's faces grew more grave. When they had tangled with Evek before they had barely survived.

Seska finally had a moment when she could open the panel access to the EPS power taps to the impulse engines. She intended to bleed the power from the accelerator/generator and vent it directly to the exhaust system.

But as the *Selva* shook under repeated impacts, she began to wonder if Gul Evek was angry enough to destroy the ship and everyone on it. Including her.

When she sat back on her heels and considered the possibility, she wasn't surprised. Not only had the ambush gone array, but she had also allowed the *Selva* to destroy the undefended Opek Nor station.

At this moment, who was her enemy? If Gul Evek didn't destroy the raider, he would take the ship in tow back to Cardassia Prime. There she would surely be tried for incompetence and imprisoned. Gul Evek would try to lay all of the blame on her, so that he wouldn't have to face similar repercussions for authorizing the Oliv ambush.

Quietly, Seska closed the panel. There was only a slim chance the raider would escape, but that was her last hope. She shuddered at the thought of remaining a Bajoran in the company of the Maquis, but that was better than death or dishonor. Barely. She would have to stay with the Maquis indefinitely, until she could redeem herself with Central Command.

Another bone-shaking impact tossed her back against the bulkhead. She slid down to sit on the floor, her head bowed to her knees. When one of the other engineers rushed by, he assured her they could handle everything, assuming she was ill. But Seska wasn't sick—she was mourning the loss of the promotion she deserved for a job well done. And she had done her job exceptionally well. Was it her fault that a freak subspace anomaly had ruined everything?

The raider shuddered, and the dim light on the bridge flickered. B'Elanna couldn't keep the ship together anymore. But she could still taste their victory. She wasn't about to let that go.

The ship was jolted over and over by at least a dozen disruptor blasts.

"Damage report!" Chakotay called out.

"Shields at 60 percent," Tuvok reported

Two lights went red. B'Elanna quickly had to reroute the fuel to injectors 3 and 4. "A fuel line has ruptured. Attempting to compensate." She opened the injectors to full, but they dropped to half-impulse power. "Dammit! We're barely maintaining impulse. I can't get any more out of it."

Chakotay was flying the raider more by the manual

controls than by computer. "Be creative," he said shortly.

Her eyes flashed. "How am I supposed to be 'creative' with a thirty-nine-year-old rebuilt engine!"

A bright orange flare erupted from the forward console. B'Elanna had to shield her eyes.

When her vision cleared, the Cardassian warship was looming over them, disruptor fire slashing out. Chakotay twisted and turned, managing to evade some of the blasts. But too many were landing on target.

B'Elanna saw the override in their communications, just as Gul Evek appeared on their screen. *"Maquis ship, this is Gul Evek of the Cardassian Fourth Order. Cut your engines and prepare to sur—"*

Chakotay cut him off before B'Elanna could. In retaliation, Evek fired another round, landing a direct hit on the bridge. One of the environmental conduits ruptured and a ceiling panel blew. Coolant billowed out in a steaming cloud.

"Initiating evasive pattern omega," Chakotay said. "Mark."

B'Elanna held on as the raider veered, overriding inertial dampers.

"Shields at 50 percent," Tuvok reported.

Chakotay turned to B'Elanna. "I need more power."

"Okay . . . ," she said, thinking fast. "Okay, take the weapons off-line. We'll transfer all power to the engines."

"Considering the circumstances," Tuvok said, "I would question that proposal at this time."

"What does it matter?" she shot back. "We're not

making a dent in their shields anyway." Chakotay glanced back at her, startled. "You wanted creative—"

He quickly checked their position on his navigation console. "Tuvok, shut down all the phaser banks." To B'Elanna, he said, "If you can give me another thirty seconds at full impulse, I'll get us into the Badlands."

"Phasers off-line," Tuvok reported.

"Throw the last photons at them and then give me the power from the torpedo systems."

"Acknowledged," Tuvok said with a real sound of respect in his voice. "Firing photons."

B'Elanna felt a rush as the raider picked up speed. Even Tuvok knew it was the right thing to do.

"Are you reading any plasma storms ahead?" Chakotay asked.

"One," Tuvok said. "Coordinates one-seven-one mark zero."

"I'm going for it," Chakotay said.

The raider banked as he changed course. The trailing edge of the ionized plasma gas could already be felt. B'Elanna noted the power feed was low to the inertial dampers, but she figured it was better to ride the bumps than to take power from the helm now.

"Plasma storm density increasing by fourteen percent," Tuvok reported. "Twenty, twenty-five—"

"Hold on," Chakotay said, teeth clenched against the shaking.

B'Elanna held her breath as they punched into the swirling plasma clouds. Electromagnetic flares whirled between the layers of thicker plasma, tinted white-gold from the contained energy. The plasma flares swirled closer, drawn by the electromagnetic energy from the *Selva*.

Chakotay banked and got around a nearby vortex. It was difficult to tell which way they were going to curve in so much whirling ionized matter.

"The Cardassian ship is not reducing power," Tuvok reported. "They are following us in."

"Gul Evek must feel daring today," Chakotay said in surprise.

B'Elanna fed more power to the inertial dampers, to give Chakotay greater directional control over the ship. He shot her a grateful glance. Their ride was still bumpy, but it no longer felt like they were out of control sliding down a muddy slope.

Chakotay banked around another plasma flare, aiming the nose upward toward the heavier plasma layer. The Cardassian ship tried to follow, but it had to veer off to avoid the flare. The warship then tried to bank in the opposite direction, but the flare whipped across the nacelle, and that section of the hull exploded.

The warship spun away. B'Elanna breathed a sigh of relief that the Cardassians were finally off their tail. The warship turned and appeared to be heading out of the plasma storms.

"They're sending out a distress signal on all Cardassian frequencies," Tuvok announced.

"Evek was a fool to take a ship that size into the Badlands," B'Elanna gloated.

"*Anyone*'s a fool to take a ship into the Badlands," Chakotay reminded her.

She exchanged a quick grin with him, then returned

to the problem of dealing with the fuel line. She would have to open up the bulkhead to get to it, so she considered leaving it until they returned to home to Terikof. Home . . . funny, but it did feel that way. Home, and with a victory in hand. . . .

Chakotay asked, "Can you plot a course through these plasma fields, Mister Tuvok?"

"The storm activity is typically widespread in this vicinity. I can plot a course, but I am afraid it will require an indirect route."

"We're in no hurry." Chakotay stood up and stretched. They had all been sitting for hours at their stations, but B'Elanna was still supervising the repair crews through her control panel.

Chakotay patted her on the shoulder, and she could feel his appreciation in the slight squeeze. She was a little uncomfortable with his reaction. She hadn't done anything special—she had just refused to give up like everyone else.

Chakotay moved to the rear, where one of the panels had blown. Another crew member had stopped the coolant leak by clamping off the junction, but Chakotay pulled out the cable with the valve to see if it could be repaired. They had already spent a fortune in coolant valves.

"I've heard Starfleet's commissioned a new *Intrepid*-class ship," B'Elanna suddenly said, knowing that she couldn't just ignore Chakotay's silent thanks. "With bioneural circuitry, to maneuver through plasma storms."

Chakotay shrugged. "We'll find a new place to hide."

She rode the bumps for a few heartbeats, trying to absorb his casual disregard. How could they give up the Terikof base? Just when she was feeling like she belonged there, with the Maquis. . . .

"You ever think about what'll happen if they catch us?" she asked quietly.

"My great-grandfather had a *poktoy,* a saying, that he passed on to my grandfather, who passed it to my father, who passed it to me." He smiled. *"Coya anochta zab."*

When she gave him a curious look, he translated, "Don't look back."

B'Elanna almost smiled. She had felt this sort of reaction before. A dead feeling inside, too painful for relief, a reaction to fighting off an attack. She tried to shrug it away. They had won. They were going home to a victory celebration—

A flash of light reflected off the bow portal, different from the usual plasma flare.

"Curious," Tuvok said thoughtfully. "We have just passed through some kind of coherent tetryon beam."

"Source?" Chakotay asked.

"Unknown," Tuvok replied.

B'Elanna got up to go see. Chakotay joined her at Tuvok's shoulder.

"Now there appears to be a massive displacement wave moving toward us," Tuvok showed them.

Amid the plasma storm indicators, there was a blur of white approaching. *Oh, no, not the subspace shock wave,* she thought. But it was moving too slowly.

"Another storm?" Chakotay asked.

"It is not a plasma phenomenon. The computer is unable to identify it."

"On screen," Chakotay ordered.

Through the layers of plasma they could see a deformation wave approaching, blanketing the red and orange and vibrant gold energy of the plasma storms.

"At current speeds," Tuvok said calmly. "It is going to intercept us in less than thirty seconds."

Chakotay moved quickly to the pilot's seat, and B'Elanna dove for hers. They were just standing there watching it bear down on them!

"Anything left in those impulse generators, B'Elanna?"

"We'll find out," she said, concentrating on her readouts, transferring power, rerouting the plasma to the driver-coil assembly.

"It is still exceeding our speed," Tuvok pointed out.

"Maximum power," Chakotay urged.

B'Elanna tried to get more. "You've got it!"

The light poured through the portal, illuminating the interior of the cockpit.

"The wave is continuing to accelerate," Tuvok informed them. "It will intercept us in eight seconds ... five. . . ."

B'Elanna had to shield her eyes as the light grew brighter and brighter. The raider was shaking so hard she thought the *Selva* would burst apart from the pressure. She couldn't see anything anymore, and suddenly everything went pure white.

Chapter Five

GUL EVEK sat glaring at the screen, hating the orange-and-gold swirls of ionized gas. As they left the plasma storm, the dense layered clouds misted over the viewscreen. They emerged into the starfield, with the ship still shaking from the trails of plasma residue.

Gul Evek was speechless with rage. But his crew knew what to do. They had powered down the antimatter reaction chamber prior to entering the plasma storms, so most of the damage was confined to the port warp nacelle. Plasma flares were known to react with the residue in the plasma injection system feeding the warp coils. The larger the vessel, the more vulnerable these systems were.

"Warp drive is probably damaged beyond repair," Agent Menet was saying. "That was pure recklessness—at a time when the Obsidian Order needs every ship!"

Agent Menet, the Obsidian Order operative on board the *Vetar,* had protested when Gul Evek ordered them into the plasma storm. But Evek would not allow the Maquis raider to slip away so easily.

Evek waved him away. "We will repair the *Vetar.* We always do."

Several of his senior officers exchanged looks, no doubt reminded of Evek's legendary persistence. He had celebrated it himself in several of his best-known epic poems, in which he described the battles he had won, and also immortalized his pursuit of the exquisite Lycoris. But that had been in his youth. . . .

"You don't know what you're doing anymore," Menet told him flatly. "You shouldn't be in command—"

Evek stood up so fast that Menet had to stumble backwards. He got right in the young idiot's face, frightening him. He could see the knowledge in Menet's eyes—Evek could kill him. Evek would have to pay for it later, but he already had much bigger mistakes to pay for.

His hand clenched into a fist, and Menet drew in his breath to cry out for help. Not that it would do him any good. Nearly everyone on the *Vetar* had suffered because of Menet's venomous reports to the Obsidian Order.

"No," Evek murmured. "You are not worth it."

As Evek turned, Menet let out a small mewing cry of relief.

Gul Evek turned his back on the agent. "You will leave the *Vetar* when the other ships arrive." He glanced around at the bridge crew, pausing to watch the interplay from their stations. Evek was not certain who had ordered the distress signal sent—probably Menek himself.

"Any of you can leave. I intend to complete my mission. That Maquis ship will not escape."

Gul Evek sat back down in the command seat to brood until the other warships arrived. They had drifted in formation, waiting uselessly for the Maquis strike force. He had been the first to leave after receiving Seska's message, but he knew the others were not far behind.

His crew were efficient, as usual, and he had a complete damage report soon after Menet scuttled from the bridge. As usual, Menet had exaggerated the situation. It would take a few days to realign the magnetic valves in the twelve plasma injectors. The arkenium-duranide lining also needed to be cleaned of the seared plasma residue left by the flare, to reduce timing discrepancies.

The exterior panels on the nacelle that had been blown off by the plasma explosion were incidental. The nacelle could operate in its skeletal condition. After they returned to port, exterior repairs could be completed.

Evek had fought both the Federation and Bajoran terrorists his entire military career. He knew how to fight, and he was good at it. He had enough seniority in military command to ensure that he would be allowed to stay in the field and hunt down the Maquis. He also knew that if he went into port he would immediately be called home to Cardassia Prime to face the consequences. It was under his recommendation that the patrols at Opek Nor had been pulled back to allow the Maquis convoy to enter their ambush. It was his responsibility that Opek Nor had been destroyed.

But he intended to make Seska pay for that mistake.

Gul Evek couldn't understand what had brought him to this dire point. He was renowned as a poet and a great soldier. He had captured the heart of the most beautiful and celebrated woman in the Cardassian empire, and Lycoris had borne him three strapping sons. His career had been worthy of legend, with Lycoris at the center of society on Cardassia Prime while he embarked on one successful war campaign after another. For over two decades, he had been one of the most powerful men in the Cardassian military.

Then, during the last several years, everything had soured. Shortly before the peace treaty with the Federation was signed, two of his sons were killed—during Starfleet's decisive defeat of a Cardassian strike force near Rabroc Nebula.

Evek had immediately requested assignment to the Demilitarized Zone, and he had actually worked with Starfleet to move colonists from the area. He was accustomed to fighting battles, but a bitter twist was added when he had to learn how to rip civilians from their homes.

Then those civilians had formed the Maquis, and had started destroying Cardassian colonies and military installations. His third son—his last living child—was killed by a Maquis raid in the Nonas system. He discovered later that the vessel belonged to Starfleet; they claimed it had been stolen, but he did not think it likely. He knew that both the Federation and Cardassia had been secretly arming their colonists.

The Maquis problem had only grown worse, but agents like Menet scoffed at the danger from these renegades. Evek had heard rumblings for the past few months among his fellow military officers in Central Command. The Obsidian Order believed the real danger lay in the Gamma Quadrant, where the Dominion ruled. They pointed to the reaction of the Federation, and the unannounced but unmistakable evacuation of people from the sectors near the Bajoran wormhole to the Gamma Quadrant.

The majority of large military vessels had been ordered to the Orias system by the Obsidian Order to prepare for a large covert campaign. It had been difficult for Gul Evek to requisition three warships along with the patrol ships to help with the ambush on the Maquis. He would have to pay for that, too. His wife had recently told him that the Obsidian Order had gained the majority of power in Central Command.

"Two warships approaching," the second in command announced. "The *Prakesh* and the *Kappet*."

"Hail Gul Dukat," Evek ordered. Dukat owed him several favors.

Gul Dukat's grim face appeared on the screen. Evek raised the eyepiece so he would not be distracted by the flow of repair reports.

"Did you get them?" Dukat asked.

Susan Wright

"The Maquis ship is in the plasma storms," Evek replied. "Once repairs are completed, we will pursue them."

Gul Dukat was disappointed. Evek could tell because Dukat's voice grew softer. "Are you sure that is wise? You're expected to report back to Central Command."

"I will report back when my mission is completed," Evek told him. "But you can take Agent Menet, and any others in my crew who wish to abandon their duty."

"I see," Dukat said slowly.

Evek was not certain Dukat would comply. It would benefit Dukat to bring in the commander who had caused the destruction of the Opek Nor station. However, it would not benefit the military in their current weakened condition for two of their best commanders to engage in battle. And Evek was not going to give up the *Vetar.* He kept his narrowed eyes on Dukat, letting his pent-up rage speak for him.

"Very well," Dukat finally said. "Send me your report and we'll complete the transfers. I must return to inform Central Command."

"Tell Lycoris—" he started to say, then broke off. "Nothing."

Dukat nodded, lifting one hand in silent agreement. Evek knew it was the last gesture of friendship that would pass between them. He could already tell by the way Dukat looked at him that his career was over. Capturing the Maquis and bringing Seska to judgment was the only slim chance he had of redirecting Central Command's rage away from himself.

"Gul Evek out," he signed off. He had never imagined he would buy his own freedom with decades of carefully built alliances.

"Arrange for the transfers," he ordered Belak, his second in command.

"Aye, sir," his second acknowledged.

Evek numbly watched as names were logged for transfer. Almost all of the new officers and those who were loyal to Menet or the Obsidian Order were leaving. For a moment he wondered if he would have a crew left to repair and operate the *Vetar.*

But the rush of names slowed and soon stopped. Nearly one-third of his crew had requested transfer off the *Vetar.* He was gratified to see that none of his senior officers had requested transfer. His best technicians remained as well. As it should be. He had always known how to reward his crew members, and they had done well under his leadership for many, many years. To serve on the *Vetar* had long been considered to be the height of many a military career.

His second saluted smartly as he handed over the final list to be signed by Gul Evek. "Gives us more room to work," Belak told Evek.

Evek smiled at Belak, feeling heartened for the first time since they had received Seska's emergency message. His crew was loyal. Why shouldn't they be? Belak's name was known throughout Cardassia because of his commander's fine poems, and his heroic deeds would live forever. Why should Belak, or Nextrom, or Salim, or any of them abandon him now? They had seen him win against all odds before.

Gul Evek straightened up in his command chair, making his plans while the transfers were completed. Then the *Prakesh* turned and gracefully departed without a final word from Gul Dukat.

"Continue with the repairs," he ordered Belak. "As soon as we can engage impulse power, set course for the Terikof system. The Maquis will have to come out of the plasma storms sometime. They'll need to head for their base."

"Aye, sir!" Belak agreed.

Gul Evek stood up, his fist hitting his palm. "We're going to find that Maquis base and destroy them. Every one of them."

Chapter Six

JANEWAY MADE a slow circuit of the bridge of *Voyager*. Finally, everything was in place. The last of the crew members had transferred on board from DS9, and the final reports had been approved. Now she could get to work.

She paced past the shoulders of her senior crew members, her first officer, Lieutenant Commander Cavit, Lieutenant Stadi, the Betazoid at helm, and young Ensign Kim at ops. Ensign Rollins commanded the security station where Tuvok, her chief of security, should be.

Janeway had not heard from Tuvok in three weeks, and that worried her. He was more than an officer under her command; Tuvok had become a trusted friend after years of working together. She was frustrated by the departure delays that had kept them from setting out for the Badlands to locate Tuvok and the Maquis raider, the *Selva.*

It's time, she thought. She nodded to First Officer Cavit.

"Lieutenant Stadi," Cavit ordered, "lay in the course and clear our departure with operations."

"Course entered," she confirmed. "Ops has cleared us."

Cavit turned to Kim at the conn. "Ready thrusters."

"Thrusters ready," Kim said, just a shade too loudly. Janeway almost smiled. He'd get his space legs and calm down soon enough.

She sat down facing the viewscreen, where the curved docking ports of DS9 could be seen. "Engage," she ordered.

As the moorings released, *Voyager* drifted away from DS9. Janeway still felt the heady excitement that came with the command of a new starship. She had felt the same thrill on leaving dock at Utopia Planetia. She liked having a home on Earth, having a life outside her duty, but she also craved to be in command of her own exploration ship, craved it so much that she had requested command of *Voyager.* The *U.S.S. Voyager* was an all-purpose ship, based out of Earth and sent to the ends of the Federation and the Gamma Quadrant on special missions.

Voyager turned, rotating the view of DS9. It was not the typical Starfleet space station. DS9 was an old Cardassian station that Starfleet had taken over after the Cardassians had left the Bajor system. Stadi lifted the ship away from the enormous curved pylon, and they swung out over the docking ring.

The Cardassians outdid themselves on this one, Janeway thought. She had never seen such a huge space station.

Now that she was in command of *Voyager,* she would probably be seeing a lot of DS9. She had had dinner the night before with Captain Benjamin Sisko, and she looked forward to working with him. She was also eager to get through that wormhole into the Gamma Quadrant. That was where the threat from the Dominion lay—and where much of their work would be done.

But first things first. The warp nacelles of *Voyager* had been designed to be able to enter plasma storms without being damaged. Janeway had been ordered to locate Tuvok and investigate the Maquis situation. After the recent destruction of Opek Nor, the Maquis had increased their raids along the Cardassian border.

"Distance, 10,000 kilometers from DS9," Kim reported.

"Engage impulse engines," Cavit ordered.

"Impulse engines on-line," Stadi confirmed.

Voyager sped into the starfield. They wouldn't be able to engage warp drive until they were clear of the Bajoran system.

Everyone was busy with their new ship . . . everyone except for Tom Paris. Paris stood awkwardly near the security station, wearing a uniform with no insignia on it, the only indicator that he was not one of her trusted officers. She caught a glimpse of his grim expression. He was an isolated island of dissatisfaction, and he had no one to blame but himself.

Janeway decided she didn't want him on her bridge. "Mister Paris, you won't be needed for twenty-four hours. Not until we arrive in the Badlands," she said shortly. "Rollins, please show Paris to his quarters."

Rollins nodded, having been fully briefed on Paris's last "assignment" in the Auckland penal colony. Rollins stepped around the security station and cordially gestured to the turbolift. "This way, Mister Paris."

Paris gave Janeway a wry glance. "Of course, *Captain.*"

She noted the sly emphasis he used on her title, and dismissed it as childish nonsense intended to provoke her. She had examined Paris's record prior to asking him to assist in locating the Maquis. He might have been a good Starfleet officer, but he had never learned to get over himself. All ego and too much energy, as far as she could tell. But none of the other captured Maquis had been willing to betray their companions, so she was making do with what she had.

Even with Paris off the bridge, his sulky shadow continued to vex her. After Rollins returned from his errand, having left Paris in his quarters, she asked, "Any problems?"

Rollins hesitated a moment too long. "No, Captain."

"Out with it," she ordered.

"He didn't make an official complaint," Rollins hedged. "So I wasn't going to mention it."

She considered dropping it, but this mission was too sensitive to take any risks. "Rollins, Cavit, in my ready room."

Janeway strode into her ready room, preferring to

stand next to the desk while Rollins and Cavit faced her. "Report," she ordered Rollins.

"Paris mentioned that he had a problem with the doctor when he checked in." Rollins shrugged slightly. "He said Starfleet officers have gotten even more obnoxious since he left the service."

"Jerk," Cavit said flatly.

"Thank you, Rollins," Janeway said. "Is that all?"

"Yes, Captain."

"You're dismissed." She waited until Rollins had left, then went over to the sofa to sit down. She gestured for Cavit to do the same.

Lieutenant Commander Cavit had served as her conn officer for several years before this posting. He was a mature, quiet man. She was glad to have him as her first officer.

"You have a problem with Tom Paris," she said, not needing to ask. She had seen Cavit's cool reception when she introduced Paris to him on the bridge.

"It's not personal," Cavit explained. "The things I've been hearing about him worry me. I don't believe he can be trusted."

"I *don't* trust him," Janeway said bluntly. "But he appears to have no loyalty to the Maquis. No loyalty to anyone. He'll give us information in order to gain his freedom."

"I don't know. . . ." Cavit shrugged doubtfully. "Maybe you should talk to the doctor. He was on Caldik Prime when it happened."

"I see," she said, finally understanding. Dr. Bist was a perfectionist, a man of no subtle grays. This morning he had posted a list of physical leisure activities the crew was ordered to choose from. Each individual was required to obtain some form of exercise at least three times a week. Janeway had privately groaned at that order, though she knew how beneficial it was for the health of the crew.

But if Dr. Bist had known Paris at the time of his court martial, he could have insights into the man's character that were not reflected in the official record.

"I'll go pay Dr. Bist a visit, now," she said. "You can handle the first status reports."

"Aye, Captain," Cavit agreed, relieved now that he had done his duty and reported a potential problem.

She valued his conscientious attitude. Dr. Bist, on the other hand, was a different matter. She was slightly disturbed on the way down to sickbay as she once again considered her new senior medical officer. Dr. Bist had not been her first—or even her fifth—choice, but he was considered to be an exceptional experimental biologist as well as a skilled surgeon. His qualifications would suit the needs of their deep-space research and reconnaissance missions.

The turbolift stopped at deck 5. As she entered sickbay, she could hear someone say, "Please state the nature of the medical emergency."

Dr. Bist and the Vulcan nurse, T'Ral, were examining a tall bald man wearing a blue medical uniform. It took a moment for Janeway to remember it was the emergency medical hologram.

"Problems, Doctor?" She wondered if she was going

to be saying that for the next week or so until they all settled into the ship.

"We're having trouble with the magnetic containment field on the EMH," Dr. Bist explained.

"Should I call engineering?" Janeway asked.

Bist dismissed T'Ral with a wave of his hand. The Vulcan immediately retreated to the medical office. "It can wait. How may I help you, Captain?"

The hologram gestured to itself. "What about me? I can't deactivate myself, you know."

Dr. Bist gave the holographic doctor a raking glance, then turned his back on it. The EMH frowned, letting out a humph! of exasperation as it folded its arms.

Janeway was even more worried. If Dr. Bist was irascible enough to even irritate a hologram, there were going to be problems on board.

"Doctor, I understand you knew Tom Paris before he was court-marshaled." She leaned against the medical bed.

"I didn't know him personally," Bist corrected. "I knew of him. Caldik Prime was a small station."

"Tell me what you do know," Janeway told him.

"He was supposed to be a good pilot. After the accident everyone treated him like a hero because he had gotten out alive." Dr. Bist tightened his lips, suddenly looking much older. "Then he admitted he had falsified his reports. He wasn't contrite, he was defiant. Like he should be thanked for finally telling the truth."

"I've noticed Mister Paris has an attitude problem," Janeway agreed.

"Confine him to quarters," Dr. Bist suggested.

"Don't let him mingle with the crew. He's not a good influence."

Janeway didn't like the doctor's tone. "I'm trying to get Mister Paris to cooperate with us. I doubt he'd be very helpful if we kept him locked up all the time."

"As you say." Dr. Bist shrugged and turned away, consulting his tricorder. Janeway could almost see him making a note to log his recommendation to the captain along with her refusal.

She didn't like having him turn his back on her that way. She was his senior officer, not a hologram. "Doctor . . ."

"Yes, is there anything else?" Dr. Bist asked over his shoulder.

"No, you're dismissed," she told him quietly.

Bist ordered the impatiently waiting hologram to hold out his arms as he scanned him with the tricorder. "T'Ral!" he called out sharply.

T'Ral appeared in the doorway of the office.

"Call engineering and get someone up here to fix this thing." The EMH looked offended, but he didn't protest this time.

Janeway left sickbay without another word. In spite of what she had seen and heard, she was confident she could handle Dr. Bist. And she was sure Mister Paris would give her no real problems.

Her only worry was Tuvok. He was an exceptional tactical officer. Yet he was either dead or involved in something he couldn't get out of. Either way, their rescue mission would undoubtedly be very dangerous.

Chapter Seven

AT FIRST, Tom Paris was determined to stay in his quarters. He wasn't going to give any other crew members a chance to dismiss him the way Dr. Bist and Captain Janeway had.

It's not that Paris expected to be welcomed with open arms, but he didn't need constant reminders of his mistake. The Federation Penal Settlement in New Zealand might look like a giant park, but he had never forgotten for a second that he couldn't leave. He hated his loss of freedom more than anything; that's why negotiating for the removal of the monitoring anklet had been important to him.

But even though Captain Janeway had agreed that the anklet could be removed, the reminders were still everywhere. He was a prisoner until he had earned his way out.

His quarters, an interior set of rooms that had a viewscreen instead of a window port, made him feel even more like a prisoner. After nearly a year of being grounded, he wanted nothing more than to look out at space—not an image of space, but space itself. Paris couldn't get enough of that view. Even the long freighter trip from Earth to Starbase 41, where Stadi had "taken custody" and ferried him to DS9, hadn't been near enough to satisfy him.

So Paris had searched out every observation lounge on *Voyager.* He must have sat for hours gazing at the stars. He had managed to avoid the thought of spending years in prison until now. Now he had a chance to get out. He would rather die than blow it again, but he had a sinking feeling that he might not be able to stop himself.

Meanwhile, crew members kept popping in to look at the observation lounges while going about their duties. They were marveling over the new ship. It even smelled new.

Some of them seemed confused to see him relaxing while everyone else was busy. Finally Paris realized he could do pretty much as he pleased, because they were all strangers to each other on this newly commissioned vessel.

After that, Paris wandered through the fifteen decks, examining the mess halls, cargo bays, escape pods, docking ports, even the shuttles in the shuttle bay. He worked his way from one end of the ship to the other. *Voyager* was top-of-the-line, with the best of everything installed in her efficient, compact design.

By the end of the first duty shift, word must have gone around because crew members began to recognize him. He was abruptly ordered from engineering when he was examining the reserve warp-core engine. Then he was denied access to the transporter room. He deliberately avoided the weapons locker, knowing that would get him into serious trouble. Janeway would probably suspect him of something stupid, like trying to hijack *Voyager*.

He ended up on deck 2, right below the bridge. The scientists in astrophysics there almost kicked him out too, but he quickly told them everything he could remember about the Badlands, describing in detail the navigational difficulties he had encountered on his one trip through the plasma storms with the Maquis.

After that, the scientists ignored him as they continued working. Paris leaned against the wall just inside the lab, where he could see the corridor. Covertly, he watched the shift change as the bridge officers came down to the officer's mess hall. The double doors were temptingly open, but when Paris saw Dr. Bist enter, he decided it wouldn't be wise to storm the citadel without reinforcements.

Paris made his move when Ensign Kim appeared, deep in a discussion with Ensign Rollins. Paris had liked Kim from the first moment he noticed that a Ferengi was trying to fleece the kid.

Paris knew that Kim would find out about him sooner or later—maybe he already had. That bothered him. The opinion of a baby ensign should have been the least of his worries, but it was easier to think about that than his real problem: What was he going to do after *Voyager* found the Maquis and he was "cut loose," as Janeway had so succinctly put it?

Neither Kim nor Rollins had noticed Paris standing in the corridor as they entered the mess hall. Ensign Kim seemed much more comfortable than he had this morning. He had spent an entire shift with his fellow officers, hammering out the last glitches in their new ship. What Paris wouldn't give for a chance to fly her. . . .

"Hi," Stadi said, joining him outside the astrophysics lab.

"Hi," he replied lightly. "I was just envying you, getting to fly *Voyager.*"

Her eyes lit up, a pilot in love with her ship. "Her reaction time is sublime."

"Well, I'll never know." Paris wished his throat hadn't made that catching sound. He was trying to keep things on the same flirtatious level they had established early on. It had been a long trip from Starbase 41, and Stadi seemed to prefer to keep things light.

She took a closer look at him. "You could try the simulation that Utopia Planetia installed in the holodeck."

"Maybe I will." Paris didn't mean to say it, but it just slipped out. "You're the first person who's talked to me like I'm a sentient life-form. To everyone else, I'm a pariah."

"I've heard of those. Aren't they some sort of Earth fish with teeth?" the Betazoid asked with a laugh.

"Sure, something like that," he agreed, thinking she

was probably closer to the truth than she knew. They treated him like he was a piranha.

Stadi hesitated. "Well, maybe I'll see you after dinner," she said lightly. "I could show you the simulation."

Paris nodded, but he didn't feel too hopeful as she entered the officer's mess. What was he doing skulking around like a puppy waiting for a handout?

Suppressing a sigh, he puckered up his lips in a whistle instead. Jamming his hands in his pockets, he headed toward the turbolift.

The door opened and Captain Janeway came out. "Glad to see you're happy with your new assignment, Mister Paris." Without another word, she entered the officer's mess.

Cheerful voices drifted through the open doorway, the talk and laughter of a satisfied crew getting to know one another, eager for adventure.

His lips were suddenly too dry to whistle anymore. Paris got onto the turbolift to head down to his quarters.

Stadi didn't want to feel Tom Paris suffering. But there was nothing she could do except reestablish her mental blocks to keep his pain from affecting her. She had been taught a long time ago on Betazed that people needed their pain in order to prompt them to act in ways that were better for them.

Tom Paris had a lot to learn, and she was a pilot, not a counselor, so it wasn't her job to help him. But she felt a twinge of remorse at leaving him standing alone in the corridor.

No, she needed to stop worrying about him. Right now she needed to concentrate on getting to know the rest of the crew. She had been on *Voyager* since they had left Utopia Planetia with the skeleton crew. Then she had left for a few days to pick up Paris at Starbase 41, so she needed to catch up and meet the newcomers.

As she turned away from the replicator with a large bowl of Kohlanese stew, Rollins gestured to her. She liked Ensign Rollins already—he was easygoing. She went to join him and the ops officer, Ensign Kim, at a table under a set of huge slanting windows.

She nodded to Kim, relieved that he was no longer as nervous as he had been earlier in the day. Her blocks were up as firmly as she could erect them, but in this sort of situation, when everyone was unsettled, it was particularly hard to maintain her emotional distance.

"Janeway just gave approval," Rollins told her. "Cavit is having a party tonight in his quarters for the senior officers."

"Perfect," she said. "I brought him a package from Starbase 41. He says it's a new recording of the Ktarian chime concert they performed at the Starbase. Maybe he'll play it for us."

Kim looked up in interest. "You like Ktarian music? So does my fiancée."

Stadi exchanged an amused glance with Rollins. "You're engaged?"

"Sure." Kim seemed embarrassed, trying to sound nonchalant. "You want to see a holo of her?"

Stadi couldn't help smiling. "Sure."

Kim pulled a slender disc from his pocket. Stadi thought it was sweet that he carried it with him.

"Her name is Libby," Kim told them.

He set it on the table and activated the sensor on the base. An image of a slender young woman appeared. She had long curly black hair and a strong intelligent brow. Her lips were as red as the tunic dress she wore, and there was something ultramodern about her, like most girls in their early twenties. Stadi suddenly felt a million years old.

"Pretty," Rollins commented. "She looks like Stadi, here, maybe ten years ago."

"Thanks a lot," Stadi said dryly. "She's lovely, Kim. You're very lucky."

"Uh, yeah," he said, confused.

She could sense his attraction to her, and she knew that he also saw her resemblance to his girl-friend.

Oh, well . . . she thought. Even if he did get a crush on her, he would get over it. At least Rollins was too seasoned to let his casual flirtation slip into something more serious.

She ate her stew and chatted with the two men. Kim was too shy to do more than examine her face when he thought she wasn't looking. Stadi gradually relaxed the tight grip on her mental blocks. Things would get better after everyone settled in.

"You're coming to the party?" Rollins asked after they were done eating.

"I have to do something first," Stadi told him. "I'll meet you there later."

Stadi stopped in the corridor, and checked to be sure no one was nearby. "Computer, location of Tom Paris?"

She wouldn't have been surprised to find that Paris was chatting up some ensign or making the moves on an available technician in the shuttle bay. But the computer replied, *"Tom Paris is currently in his quarters on deck 5."*

She wasn't sure why she cared, but she did. Maybe because he so desperately needed a friend. She certainly couldn't give him what he needed, but she could help him get through his first evening on board. She would hate to be as lonely as he was.

Since she wasn't familiar with the ship, it took a few minutes to find his quarters. She buzzed on the door, and there was a short pause before he answered, *"Yes? Who is it?"*

"It's Lieutenant Stadi," she called through the door. "Do you want to try the *Voyager* simulation?"

The door opened into a dark room. "Lights up," Paris said. He was standing in the doorway to the bedroom.

"I'm sorry, I didn't realize you had gone to sleep," she told him.

"No, not at all." He smoothed down his uniform top. "I'd love to try the simulation. I haven't flown a ship for over a year. . . ."

Stadi liked him better this way, even though it was clear he was aching inside. At least he wasn't trying to cover it up with warp-speed flirtation.

"Come on, then," she told him. They left his room and started toward the holodeck. "They've installed a top-grade Starfleet simulator in this ship. The bioneural network enhances the realistic response pattern."

She kept the conversation on conversion speeds and various navigational techniques. Paris seemed grateful to discuss flying with a fellow pilot.

She had reserved holodeck 2. It responded to her voice command. "Load *Voyager* navigation simulation." She glanced at him appraisingly. "Level 4."

Paris snorted, but he didn't protest. He had probably been a hot-shot level 10 at the Academy, but she didn't need to point out that his reaction response would be affected by his lack of flight time.

The door opened to reveal a perfect replica of the bridge of *Voyager*. Paris stepped inside, looking around in frank admiration. He had been much more reserved when she had seen him on the real bridge this morning.

"Do you want crewmembers?" she asked.

"No," he said quickly. "I like it this way."

He went to the conn, his hands resting on the back of the chair as he looked down at the navigational console.

"Have a seat," Stadi urged, turning the chair for him.

Paris didn't take his eyes off the control panel. The simulation had automatically loaded her preferred display layout. Stadi started pointing out features, and he began tapping the panel before she was done explaining.

Stadi smiled as she pulled back. Paris was almost in a trance, getting a feel for the ship. The viewscreen showed them at dock at DS9, having selected the ship's last known port. Paris entered the coordinates for the

Badlands and proceeded through the operations sequence.

She almost expected him to pull some fancy docking maneuver to show off in front of her. But he broke contact with the docking pylon and smoothly engaged thrusters to gently push the ship away from the station. Exactly as if it were real, not a simulation.

His expression was rapt as he fired aft thrusters, pushing them further away. At 10,000 kilometers, the prescribed distance from any stationary object, he engaged impulse engines.

"Nice . . . ," he murmured, overriding the computer and engaging the manual controls. He tried different flight patterns as they flew through the illusionary Bajoran system. "Handles like a much smaller ship."

"But she has real power," Stadi said, leaning over the seat. "Take her up to warp 9."

His eyes met hers, and they both laughed. "Warp 9 it is!"

Paris engaged warp speed and moved up the scale until they reached warp 9. Stadi could almost feel the shift in the simulation as their speed increased. This was the best flight simulator she had ever flown, and Paris seemed to agree.

As they laughed together and talked about *Voyager,* she realized she wasn't just doing this for him. She had longed to share this fantastic ship with someone who was as passionate about flying as she was.

"She's fast!" Paris exclaimed. "You can feel it in the—"

Suddenly there was a power interruption. The simulation fluttered and broke for a moment, revealing a glimpse of the yellow hologrid.

Stadi froze. "End simulation!"

The bridge dissolved around them, but Stadi was too busy sensing the real motion of *Voyager* to pay any attention. "We've dropped out of warp."

The red-alert klaxon began to flash.

"I've got to get to the bridge," she told Paris. As she ran out of the holodeck, the last thing she saw was Paris standing alone in the middle of the yellow hologrid, looking like he had lost everything in the world.

Chapter Eight

ENSIGN KIM was the first one to arrive at Lieutenant Commander Cavit's party. He felt very awkward, so he offered to leave, which made Cavit look at him like he was crazy. Kim cringed inside as Cavit went to fetch him a synthehol.

Dr. Bist arrived next, which made things worse. Kim had never heard of Dr. Bist before he boarded, but his crewmates had been quick to tell him about the man's reputation for activist work. He had been instrumental in getting medical supplies and training to the non-Federation Delores system after the colonies were hit by a cosmic string fragment. According to Cavit, Dr. Bist was one of the most respected physicians in Starfleet. Kim was willing to take their word for it. All he knew so far was that the doctor had to be one of the most abrasive men in Starfleet.

Kim didn't have anything to say to him. Especially after this morning, when the doctor had so snidely instructed him to check in with the captain. And Bist had been positively rude to Tom Paris.

Kim nodded to the doctor, and was relieved when Cavit sat down to talk to Bist. Kim knocked back his entire glass of synthehol, hoping it would relax him. Where was Rollins? Where was Stadi? Not that he especially wanted to see Stadi. . . .

Suddenly the red-alert klaxon began to sound. The computer announced, *"Red alert."*

Kim was so surprised that he crushed the cup in his hand. Shards of glass fell to the carpet, but Lieutenant Commander Cavit didn't even notice. He was already running to the door. "Move it, Ensign!"

Dr. Bist was frowning, and he gave Kim a raking glance. Hastily, Kim brushed off the last of the glass onto the table before following Cavit to the bridge. He could feel the grooves in his palm from the rough edges. His first real red alert, and he had panicked.

His heart was pounding in the turbolift. What would it be? Engine malfunction? Surely they weren't being attacked on his first day of duty . . . He felt the full weight of his seniority, and he suddenly knew why it was such a rare thing that he had been made an ops officer on board a starship right out of Starfleet Academy . . . A lot of his fellow cadets had been openly envious.

His palms were sweating as he took over his station. But Starfleet training was good: he went through the

Susan Wright

routine checklist as the other bridge officers took their stations.

"Full stop," Janeway ordered, as soon as she stepped onto the bridge.

"Dropping out of impulse," Stadi confirmed from the helm.

"Report," Janeway said, turning to Kim.

"Sensors indicate that a subspace shockwave impacted *Voyager*, Captain. It lasted .7 seconds. Sensors were unable to track the trajectory of the subspace wave."

The engineering officer confirmed, "The warp field was disrupted. Warp drive startup sequence is underway."

Janeway nodded shortly. "What was the source of the subspace wave?" she asked Kim.

The computer was just finishing its comparison, and Kim read directly from the readout. "It's the Badlands anomaly, sir . . . m'am," he quickly amended.

He glanced up to see that the others were as surprised as he was. They had all heard about unlucky crews who had encountered the subspace anomaly near the Badlands.

"We were exposed to tetryon radiation?" Janeway asked.

Initiating the technique recommended by Commander Data of the *Enterprise*-D, Kim scanned for tetryon particles. "The exposure was minimal, 50 rads at most. We must be further away than previously recorded encounters."

"We're still some distance from the plasma storms,"

80

Janeway said thoughtfully. "I thought the Badlands anomaly was found much closer to the plasma storms."

"I'll alert sickbay to watch for tetryon radiation," Cavit said quietly. "Just in case."

Kim agreed with Captain Janeway. They were barely inside the Badlands sector. The end of Kamiat Nebula was on the viewscreen, twisting into the distance. The blue-and-white gases were brilliant against the starfield, deceptively benign-looking. But a Starfleet warning appeared on Kim's console that Kamiat Nebula was sometimes used as cover by Maquis ships. He scanned it carefully and found no energy signatures.

"No ships within long-range sensors, Captain," Kim reported. He blushed to think of his garbled "sir— m'am." When would he get it right?

Janeway nodded. "Stand down to yellow alert, and continue on course, full impulse power. Let me know when warp drive is available." She started toward the science station on the port side. "I want to find out more about this Badlands anomaly."

The science station was just in front of Kim's station, along the side of the bridge. Leaning over the science officer, Janeway began an animated discussion of asymmetrical spatial distortions and tetryon particles. Kim could overhear pieces of their conversation as he monitored the routing of power to the main systems from impulse drive.

"Since tetryons only exist in subspace," Janeway mused quietly, "the presence of tetryon radiation is usually indicative of an intrusion of subspace into normal space."

"Such as the formation of a subspace rift," the science officer agreed.

"Now what would cause a subspace rift?" Janeway mused, "And one that occurs randomly, at that."

Obligingly, the science officer suggested various sources. "Tetryon emissions were sent by solanagen-based aliens into the *Enterprise*-D cargo bay in 2369. Tetryon particles are also found near cloaked vessels. Natural tetryon fields occur regularly in the Hekaras system. . . ."

Kim was distracted when the communications grid was activated on the frequencies customarily used by Cardassians. "Captain! We're receiving a distress signal. It's from a Cardassian warship, the *Vetar.*"

Janeway strode back to the command chair. "On screen."

A Cardassian appeared on the viewscreen, his face deeply lined. Kim couldn't have imagined a more battle-worn commander.

"*This is Gul Evek. Emergency assistance is required.*" He seemed to force the words out, as if it took almost more strength than he had.

Kim boosted power to the communications grid to compensate. The *Vetar* was barely projecting a signal.

"This is Captain Janeway of the Starship *Voyager,*" the captain replied. "Give us your coordinates and we will respond immediately."

Gul Evek nodded shortly to someone out of sight. "*These are our coordinates and crew complement. The* Vetar *is on emergency power. Structural integrity and life-support systems are failing. We estimate less than one hour before catastrophic failure."*

"What happened?" Janeway asked.

"We were hit by a subspace shockwave. We had to eject the warp core during a breach."

"The Badlands anomaly. We felt it, too," Janeway told him. "But we suffered no damage."

Ensign Kim cautiously interjected, "Captain, we've received the coordinates. Bearing three-three-zero mark fifteen." He routed the information to navigation.

"Captain, at warp 4 we can intercept in less than one hour," Stadi offered.

Janeway glanced back at the engineering station. The chief engineer reported, "Warp drive will be on-line in a few moments, Captain."

Janeway nodded. "We're on our way, Gul Evek."

The Cardassian stiffly inclined his head. The image disappeared.

"Notify Starfleet that we're engaging in a rescue mission to the *Vetar,*" Janeway ordered Kim.

"Aye, Captain!" he acknowledged.

Some of the bridge crew, Lieutenant Commander Cavit and the science officer in particular, seemed worried about the rescue mission. Cavit even ordered Rollins to raise shields to maximum as they went to warp 3, and to secure engineering and weapons.

But Kim knew that attitudes about the Cardassians had been gradually changing since the truce was established five years ago. Starfleet was cooperating with the Cardassians with regard to the Maquis, who had banded together to fight the 2370 treaty establishing the new border between the Cardassian Empire and the Federation. Despite constant conflict with the Maquis, or perhaps because of it, relations between the Cardassian Empire and the Federation were good for the first time in their long history of warfare.

Kim was so interested in the topic that several months earlier, while still at the Academy, he had researched the claims made by the Maquis. The resulting article in the Academy newspaper had gotten a lot of attention, sparking debates among the cadets and officers of Starfleet. He had occasionally wondered if that infamous article had influenced his posting on *Voyager*. And now, his first day on duty, he was going to meet Cardassians face-to-face. This is what he had worked and trained for. He just hoped he wouldn't let anyone down.

Captain Janeway went to her ready room to examine the information available on Cardassian operations in the area—and to find out more about Gul Evek. Her first officer had been actively involved in the Cardassian war, which tended to make Cavit extracautious about interacting with them. But Janeway preferred to arm herself with information rather than shields.

Scanning the computer record, she realized why she had recognized the name. Aman Evek was the great Cardassian poet, one of the modern soldier-artists who had helped generate a renaissance of romantic literature in the Cardassian Empire. She had always known he was a fine poet, but his military record was impressive as well, especially during the years of the war with the Federation.

Since the truce, Evek had been a constant presence in the Demilitarized Zone. Gul Evek had been at Dorvan V when the Native American colonists refused to evacuate. Gul Evek and Captain Picard had been instrumental in reaching a mutually beneficial agreement, whereby Federation colonists agreed to become Cardassian colonists, subject to Cardassian rule.

Yet just last year, Captain Sisko had accused Gul Evek of secretly providing arms to Cardassian colonists in the Demilitarized Zone in direct violation of the Federation-Cardassian treaty. No conclusive evidence had been found in that case.

However, two months later, Gul Evek brought charges against Miles O'Brien, chief of operations on DS9, for illegally shipping arms to the Maquis. It was the same charge that had been leveled against him by Starfleet. In an almost unprecedented move, the verdict against O'Brien by the Cardassian court was set aside by Central Command, and O'Brien was released. Additional details were not provided.

Janeway could tell from the available data that Gul Evek was not above deceiving Starfleet in order to gain the advantage. Janeway leaned forward and signaled the bridge, "Cavit, scan the *Vetar* as soon as we're in range. I want confirmation that she's disabled."

"*Acknowledged,*" he replied, approval in his tone.

"When will the closest Cardassian ship arrive?" she asked.

"Not for eleven standard hours," Cavit told her. *"There appears to be a lack of Cardassian presence in the Badlands sector."*

"Understood. Continue scanning on long-range sensors for other Cardassian vessels."

Janeway spent the intervening time giving orders to her crew to prepare them to evacuate a *Galor*-class warship. Gul Evek reported that there were 130 crew members on board the *Vetar,* almost the same crew complement as *Voyager.* Finding room for everyone would be difficult. They moved shuttles into the repair rooms to clear the shuttle bay, and some of the crew doubled up to make quarters available for the officers of the *Vetar.* Even cramped quarters would be far more comfortable than the tiny escape pods.

Janeway also made sure security was on alert and had secured not only engineering but the bridge and the computer core, with its sensitive neural gel packs. With over a hundred Cardassians on board, it would be easy for them to take over the ship if they chose. But refusing to evacuate them would violate the most fundamental principle of space law.

As they neared the *Vetar,* Janeway returned to the bridge to hear the senior officer's reports.

"Their shields and weapons systems are off-line," Rollins reported. "We're reading emergency power only."

"Magnify image," Janeway ordered.

The *Vetar* appeared on the viewscreen. It was motionless against the starfield, and to her experienced eye, appeared to be adrift. The exterior lights were off, with only a few reddish spots along the front. The warp nacelles were dead. It was such a large ship to look so defenseless. Not for the first time, Janeway wondered why there were only 130 crew members on board a ship that normally had a compliment of close to two hundred.

"The exterior of the warship has been extensively scored by plasma," Kim reported. "The warp core was recently ejected. I'm reading heavy antimatter residue in the area, probably from a warp-core breach."

"Any other vessels in the area?" she asked.

"Nothing on long-range sensors, Captain."

Janeway took her seat. "Bring us into transporter range. Shields on maximum until I give the order."

The captain kept a close eye on the sensor readouts. She was watching for any spike in the energy level that would indicate the *Vetar* was a threat.

"Open hailing frequencies," she ordered.

The head and shoulders of Gul Evek appeared. There was a haze in the air obscuring the image, and he coughed before he spoke. "Good, you've arrived. There's not much time left."

"We're ready to transport your crew on board, Commander."

Gul Evek grimaced. "Many of my crew are . . . injured."

"Tetryon radiation poisoning?" Janeway was not surprised after reading the reports filed by the *Enterprise* and the *Enterprise*-D.

Evek wearily nodded. "Over one-third of my crew

has been struck down. More are weakening every moment. We can't hold the ship together anymore."

"We'll begin transporting you to *Voyager* immediately," she informed him. "Request permission to send medical teams to the *Vetar* to assist in the evacuation."

Gul Evek pulled back slightly, instinctively reacting against the idea of allowing Starfleet personnel on board his ship. It reminded Janeway of her own reservations about allowing the Cardassians to board *Voyager*.

Then he sagged forward again, glancing around in resignation at his disabled ship. "I will send you the transport coordinates."

"My first officer, Lieutenant Commander Cavit, will lead the rescue team." She nodded to Cavit, who acknowledged and left the bridge.

Janeway didn't know what else to say to Gul Evek. She no longer had any doubts that this was indeed a true emergency. The knowledge that he was about to abandon ship was seared too deeply into the commander's eyes.

When the general announcement went out, calling for crewmembers trained in emergency medical triage, Paris went to the transporter room on the off-chance that he would be allowed to help. He was one of only twenty crew members who arrived.

First Officer Cavit took one look at him and sneered, "What do you think you're doing?"

"I can help," Paris replied stiffly. "I had emergency medical training at the Academy."

Cavit ordered him, "Report to sickbay. You'll make a good stretcher bearer."

"Now wait a minute—" Paris started to protest.

"Just give me a reason," Cavit warned, "one reason to confine you to quarters."

Paris felt his face burning as the others stared at him. He left as Cavit was dividing them into teams of four to assist in evacuating Cardassians from their ship.

Paris was tempted to call it quits. He would rather not have to report to Dr. Bist. He wondered if everyone else who had been stationed at Caldik Prime felt the same way about him, or if it was just the sanctimonious doctor. Probably everyone.

But he didn't want to give Cavit the satisfaction by returning to his quarters. So Paris went to sickbay. With everyone else rushing around, he wanted something to do.

Sickbay was in an uproar. Dozens of volunteers were taking orders from Dr. Bist. "One-third of the medical escort teams will bring the injured Cardassians from the transporter rooms to sickbay for triage. The rest will escort patients to the upper cargo bays on deck 7 that have been converted into wards. Leave the uninjured Cardassians to the security volunteers. They will be taken to temporary housing in the main shuttle bay."

The man's officiousness got on Paris's nerves. "Where do you want me?" he called out. "I have medical training."

Dr. Bist almost snarled, but the lack of medical volunteers was clear. "Stay here and assist the emergency medical hologram. I'll be in transporter room one doing triage on the most severely injured. Nurse T'Ral is in charge in the cargo bays. The rest of you, report to the transporter rooms."

They practically ran, snapped into action by Dr. Bist's sharp order.

Dr. Bist didn't wait for everyone to clear out. "Activate the emergency medical hologram."

Paris drew back as a tall balding man in a Starfleet medical uniform appeared right next to him. The tiny sickbay was too crowded.

"Please state the nature—" the hologram recited. He broke off, eyeing the crush as everyone tried to leave sickbay at once.

"Hiya," Paris told the hologram. "Popular place you got here."

"Apparently not," the hologram countered dubiously, noting that everyone was frantically trying to leave. "Please state the nature of the medical emergency."

Dr. Bist didn't bother with courtesies. "Approximately forty Cardassians will arrive in the next few minutes. They were injured by tetryon radiation."

"Did you say *forty* Cardassians?" the hologram repeated, glancing around the four-biobed facility. "There's not enough *standing* room in here for forty people."

"The stretcher bearers will take them to temporary wards or the shuttle bay after you've treated them." Dr. Bist sniffed as he looked at the hologram. "The EMH, of course, must stay here. You'll work with Tom Paris. My other medical technicians will be in the cargo bays where most of the injured will be bedded down."

Paris gave the EMH a slight shrug. Clearly, Dr. Bist didn't like either of them.

"Understood, Doctor," the hologram replied quite professionally. He immediately went over to the medical equipment module to begin loading hyposprays. He held the first one out when he was done.

Paris was busy watching Dr. Bist gather his large medical kit, until the EMH pointedly said, *"Nurse . . . hypospray."*

"Oh, right." Paris took it from him. Then he laid it on one of the trays, as he had been taught at the Academy.

Now that he thought about it, he could hardly remember anything from his semester of medical triage training . . . except for that sweet Denebian who had been in the same class. He had spent more time whispering in her ear than listening to the lectures on traumatic injuries.

"Uh, by the way," he told the hologram. "I'm not a nurse. I can barely operate a biobed."

The EMH rolled his eyes. "What is Starfleet coming to?"

"It's an unusual situation," Paris pointed out. "It's not every day we evacuate a Cardassian warship."

"I was invented for *unusual* situations," the hologram retorted. "However, we must strive to maintain a level of professional quality at all times."

Paris raised his hands as if to ward off the hologram's sanctimonious speech. "Let me guess—Dr. Bist programmed your personality routines."

"No," the annoyed hologram retorted. "I was programmed by Dr. Lewis Zimmerman at Jupiter Station."

"Oh, yeah. Now that you mention it, I see a resemblance."

The hologram looked vaguely offended, but he didn't have time to reply. The first Cardassian casualties began to arrive.

The EMH moved rapidly, scanning the injured and injecting cysteamine into their neck ridges. Paris helped them into beds and quickly learned how to perform a cellular regeneration sweep. Their skin seemed to be cold to the touch, but he wasn't sure if that was a sign of sickness or normal Cardassian physiology.

He only had a few minutes with each one while giving them the regeneration treatment. Then they were helped or carried off to the temporary wards where they could lie down.

Paris didn't mind treating the Cardassians. He had never carried a personal grudge against them, unlike many of the Maquis. He had only joined the Maquis because he couldn't find another job. Private transport companies wouldn't hire someone who had been cashiered out of Starfleet for pilot error resulting in the death of three fellow officers. And he didn't have any credit to buy his own craft to set up a ferry business.

He had hoped to build up a stash through a little mercenary work. What a great idea *that* had been—he'd been caught and sent straight to the penal settlement on Earth.

After his first few Cardassian patients, Paris decided he shouldn't try to switch careers and become a medical technician. He was awkward with the regenerator and he didn't know what to say to the patients looking up at him, gasping for breath through the pain. It was strange to see such large, powerful people reduced to feebleness, looking so confused and vulnerable.

In between waves of patients, he had a moment to comment to the emergency medical hologram, "They act like they've never been in a medical bed before." His arms ached from pushing burly Cardassians back down, including the women, though most of them couldn't have stood up on their own.

"The Cardassians have a minimalist approach to medicine," the EMH replied. "Leave the patient alone—if they die they weren't strong enough to live."

"No wonder they're all afraid of us," Paris said.

Another wave of evacuees arrived. Paris was beginning to see a pattern of long-term physical stress and strain appearing on the monitors of the biobeds.

"You been out a long time?" he asked one young Cardassian as he worked the regenerator. He had only received 250 rads.

The Cardassian glanced nervously to both sides, but his fellow crew members were too sick to listen if they wanted to.

"I can tell from the scan." Paris recognized a fellow rebel. "What's been going on?"

"A third of our crew left," the Cardassian whispered, "We've been working shorthanded since then, searching for the Maquis vessel."

"Why?" Paris asked. "What happened?"

"They destroyed Opek Nor." The Cardassian seemed to gain strength from his outrage. "They killed over a hundred . . . our friends. . . ."

"The Maquis did that?" Paris was impressed in spite of himself. Opek Nor was a prime strategic facility.

"One ship," the Cardassian said bitterly. "One ship got through the planetary defense system. Then they disappeared into the Badlands. The *Vetar* went in after them."

Paris whistled. "A *Galor*-class warship went into the plasma storms?"

"Our warp nacelle picked up a plasma flare. Practically crushed the ship." He grimaced as he shifted positions. "We repaired the *Vetar* and were searching the nearby systems. Then that subspace shockwave came out of nowhere—"

The EMH appeared by Paris's side. "This is no time for casual conversation, Mister Paris. We have patients to attend to."

Paris realized he had stopped using the regenerator. Hastily he began passing it over the Cardassian.

The hologram squinted at the readings. "He's done. Take this man to the shuttle bay." The doctor turned and called out, "Next!"

The Cardassian was helped away before Paris could learn his name or rank. He continued to go from one bed to the next, regenerating each Cardassian. Soon their weary eyes and remote expressions began to blend together.

Paris was curious to know more about what had

happened, but it seemed like too much of an intrusion to question these haunted people. The one time he tried to ask about the Maquis ship that had struck down Opek Nor, there was such pain in the officer's voice that he patted her shoulder and told her to not speak anymore.

Chapter Nine

AS A COURTESY, Janeway went to the transporter room
to greet Gul Evek. He was the last Cardassian to beam
aboard, after the other 128 crew members of the *Vetar*
had been evacuated. Many had already received medical treatment. According to Dr. Bist's preliminary report, nearly seventy were seriously injured, with at
least one-third of those reading tetryon irradiation in
excess of 600 rads. They would have to be monitored
carefully and receive cellular regeneration on a regular
basis in order to fully recover.

"The *Vetar* is evacuated and secured," Lieutenant
Commander Cavit reported. He had accompanied the
commander of the warship back to *Voyager.* "Gul
Evek," he said, performing the introduction, "this is
Captain Janeway."

Janeway nodded in respect. "Welcome aboard, Gul

Evek. We're honored to receive such a renowned commander of the Cardassian Empire."

He looked at her sharply, as if he hadn't expected her to know him. Cavit noted her conversational manner and backed away, leaving the transporter room when he received her nod of dismissal.

"I've read some of your poetry," she told Gul Evek. "I've always followed the romantic literary trends of our day. Your *Long Voyage to Hutet* has been a favorite of mine since it was translated."

"Thank you, Captain Janeway." His eyes were hollow, surrounded with purple smudges. "You are generous to take in my crew."

"Not at all. If *Voyager* had been slightly ahead of schedule, we would have suffered the same fate as you." She smiled gently. "I believe you would have done the same for us."

"Of course," he said automatically.

She could tell that he was nearly stretched to the breaking point.

Dr. Bist chose that moment to step in and scan Gul Evek, without even asking for permission. "A relatively low exposure, 100 rads. Very lucky considering—"

"Thank you," Janeway told Bist, "that will be all." Trying to soften the effect of the doctor's brusque manner, she gestured to the door of the transporter room. "This way to your quarters, Commander."

"I would like to check on my crew," he told her.

"Very well," Janeway agreed. "We can go down to the cargo bays where most of your injured are quartered."

Janeway paused at the transporter console to make sure Ensign Kim had stabilized the forcefield that stretched around the *Vetar*. The warship was no longer able to maintain structural integrity on its own. Kim confirmed that the warship was in tow as they continued toward the Badlands at full impulse power.

Janeway noted Kim's final report, and told Gul Evek, "The *Prakesh* is on her way to pick up your crew."

She thought he flinched at the name, but she wasn't sure. Gul Evek was silent as they toured the sick wards where Dr. Bist and Nurse T'Ral were treating the Cardassians. It was very quiet in the wards, with little movement or sound from the injured. Gul Evek spoke to no one, but his crew saw him. Some looked away.

Then they went down to the main shuttle bay, where rows of cots had been set up for the crewmembers who were uninjured. Gul Evek spoke briefly to Nextrom, the commanding officer in the shuttle bay.

Janeway drew away slightly, glad to see that most of the Cardassians in the shuttle bay were either eating or resting comfortably. They were much more alert than the injured crew members in the cargo bay. But the way they looked at Gul Evek struck her deeply. Could losing a ship explain the despair she sensed?

Gul Evek finished a discussion with his senior officer. "I am finished here," he told Janeway.

"We have quarters for you on deck 3," Janeway informed Evek. "Your officers are free to go into unrestricted areas. However we would prefer it if the majority of your crew stayed here in the shuttlebay."

"That is acceptable," Gul Evek told her.

Janeway showed him to the guest quarters that had been reserved for the Cardassian commander. She pointed out the replicator and reminded him that he would have to report to sickbay soon for cellular regeneration.

Before she left, Janeway said, "I understand you patrol the Badlands sector. We're looking for a Maquis ship that's been seen in this area. She's called the *Selva*."

Gul Evek quickly turned and with several strides was right in her face. "The *Selva!* What do you know about that ship?"

His sudden aggression was so startling that Janeway prepared to defend herself. "It's a Maquis raider that has been seen in the area." The captain firmly held Gul Evek's gaze, standing her ground. She wasn't about to reveal that a Starfleet spy was on board, much less her security chief. "You obviously know this ship."

"Know it!" he exclaimed bitterly. "You heard about the destruction of Opek Nor a few weeks ago?"

"Yes," she admitted. The reports had come through the usual channels. "The Maquis claimed credit for it."

"The *Selva* destroyed Opek Nor."

Janeway froze. She hadn't put the two together because she had received the information about Opek Nor long after Tuvok had missed several rendezvous. "What happened to the *Selva?*"

"We destroyed it." he growled. "We pursued it into the plasma storms."

Janeway willed herself not to draw back. The man was acting irrationally.

Gul Evek turned away so she could no longer see his face. "The *Vetar* was almost destroyed by a plasma flare," he finally told her. "We have looked for them, day after day, but they must have been destroyed."

Janeway felt somewhat better. If he hadn't seen it happen, then he could be wrong. "Well, we would appreciate their last known coordinates so we can check."

He must have heard her skepticism. "I have a contact among the Maquis who claims the *Selva* never returned to their base. They are mourned as dead by the Maquis."

Janeway felt something twist in her chest, thinking of Tuvok, hoping that it was not true. "Nevertheless, we would appreciate the coordinates."

"You can't take this ship into the plasma storms," he told her. "It's too big."

"*Voyager* was designed to enter the plasma storms," Janeway told him.

His eyes widened, as if thinking of the possibilities that offered. "You intend to track them down, don't you?"

"That's my mission," she agreed. "I'm not going to stop until I find the *Selva*."

"Then I will give you the coordinates," he told her.

"Good." She started for the door, but turned back. "Oh, and if you can also give us any sensor logs you obtained on the subspace shockwave, that would be helpful. We can't allow this thing to keep destroying our starships."

"No, I suppose you can't. Go ahead, take them," he agreed as if distracted by thoughts of the Maquis. "The *Selva* also encountered the tetryon shockwave shortly before they attacked Opek Nor."

"They did?" Janeway almost asked how he knew, but she already did. His "contacts" in the Maquis must keep him well informed. "We would like any information you obtained about that as well."

"The data is in these logs." Gul Evek patted the bag hanging from his shoulder. "I will send it to you right away."

"Thank you. As I said, your officers are free to go about the unrestricted areas of the ship. You'll find your senior officers quartered on this deck."

Gul Evek nodded, but he seemed too dispirited to do anything but stand there, clearly waiting for her to leave.

"If you need anything," she told him. "Feel free to contact me at any time."

He didn't bother to reply. As the door shut behind her, she couldn't help thinking about his expression. It seemed as if he could hardly focus through the fatigue and pain. No, she could not imagine what he was feeling right now. And she hoped she never would know what it was like to evacuate her ship.

Gul Evek was not certain how long he had been standing in the center of the room, so different from his quarters on the *Vetar*. Everything was different now.

Finally he sat down, the bag of isolinear rods on his lap. Duty still called; he needed to copy the pertinent information to Captain Janeway. There was something about her determined look that made him certain she would continue his mission. It was her security officer, Tuvok, who had been spying on board the *Selva*. She had good reason to search down that ship. And once she found it, the Maquis on board would be brought to justice.

Methodically he went through his logs for the past several weeks, isolating passages that pertained to the *Selva*. He was tempted for a moment to reveal that Seska was a Cardassian spy, but he could not betray his training. Starfleet would soon discover Seska was a Cardassian with their medical checks. Then, maybe, she would get the punishment she deserved for the lives she had destroyed. Including his.

He loaded the data onto an isolinear chip and sent it through the computer system to Captain Janeway. Then he requested permission to send his report to Central Command. Janeway herself notified him to proceed.

Gul Evek stiffly made his report about the evacuation of the *Vetar*. As a poet, he was so accustomed to choosing his words carefully that the habit remained with him still. But there were no ringing statements, no grand conclusions this time.

Evek sent it, along with a copy of the data he had given Captain Janeway. He had divulged no sensitive information, and this would forestall suspicions that he had violated military protocol.

With the message sent, he made sure the log bag was neatly ordered. He intended to take it to Belak, his first officer. Then he noticed a smaller message rod in his private slot, and he slowly pulled it out.

The message had arrived shortly before the *Vetar* was struck by the subspace shockwave. It was from his wife Lycoris. He had viewed it once, and had been stunned from that blow when the shockwave hit—and his life truly ended. The two seemed indelibly linked in his mind.

He slipped the slender rod into the Starfleet computer slot. After a few beeps, it was accepted and interfaced. The image of Lycoris appeared on the monitor.

It was little things he noticed, this time. The perfect folds of her gown draping from one shoulder to her knee as she sat on a decorative bench. The wall behind her was a deep green, the perfect compliment to her verdant coloring. He leaned closer and could see the careful makeup used to enhance her seductive features.

She had made herself look perfectly beautiful to say, "I cannot live this way any longer, Aman Evek. We are disgraced, and the outrage over Opek Nor continues on Prime. I cannot save myself as well as you. So I must save myself." Her eyes stayed steady on the screen, her perfect mouth forming the words. "I have begun proceedings to separate."

Lycoris went on, giving details of estates and settlements, but Evek simply watched her hand turn as she raised it for emphasis, the way she moved her head, so graceful yet deliberate . . . A hard, cold woman, putting an end to decades of a life shared together. And what a glorious life it had been.

"I had intended to wait until you returned." Lycoris hesitated. He could almost see her thinking that it was likely he would be immediately interned and tried for his crimes. She would never have to see him again. "But I cannot endure this pain any longer."

She didn't say farewell. And her eyes never wavered, never softened with the remembrance of love past.

As the image faded, and their family seal appeared to signal the end of the message, Evek almost expected to feel the world turn on end, as it had before—when the subspace shockwave created a weightless state that seemed to last an eternity. He had let himself go, ceasing to struggle against the upheaval.

But then he had had to deal with the aftermath of the disaster and the wreck of the *Vetar*. Now he sat in this silent room, feeling only the thrumming of *Voyager*'s powerful systems, hearing only the high-pitched whine of distant servos.

After a long time he stood up, every muscle protesting. He took the log bag and slung it over his shoulder again, keeping the last message from Lycoris in his hand.

In the corridors, he saw no Cardassians. He knew that if he were in their place, part of the broken crew of a broken commander, he would hole up somewhere until the dust settled. Thankfully, his disgrace would not become their burden. They were not responsible for the mistakes he had made. Only Seska was to blame.

His first officer had quarters not far from his. Gul Evek handed over the log bag to Belak. "You keep the logs."

Belak accepted the bag, his mouth working in an effort to remain at attention. "Commander, what are your orders?"

"Make sure the crew is prepared to transfer to the *Prakesh*," Evek ordered. "You will lead them, Belak."

"Acknowledged, Commander." He held his salute until Evek returned it.

After that, Evek couldn't return to his quarters. The colors were too varied and brilliant. It didn't feel right. He wanted the *Vetar*, so he searched until he found an observation lounge that overlooked his ship. *Voyager* seemed very small as she hovered over the warship, protecting it with her own integrity field.

Though the *Vetar* was in tow, it did not look badly damaged. The skeletal frame of the warp nacelle was the worst scar. A month in space dock and she would be nearly as good as new. He wondered who would command her next, and he silently wished the unknown gul great success.

If only there were some way he could redeem himself. He had been considering the possibility of taking over *Voyager* ever since he'd heard she could maneuver through the plasma storms. The ship was strong enough to stabilize the warship and still proceed at full impulse power . . . It would be quite a coup to obtain this ship for Cardassia.

It would also start an interstellar war and turn his crew into renegades.

His mind was so numb that it was difficult to try to strategize. Instead, he watched the *Vetar* being pulled along and thought about his first years in command.

The *Vetar* had been a pristine *Galor*-class warship back then, the best in the fleet. He had written the *Ode to Lycoris* during those early days, when their courtship was in full bloom.

He turned the rod over in his hands, thinking of the beautiful Lycoris. She was past her prime perhaps, but still an exquisite woman. She would survive his disgrace and go on to be praised and petted by Cardassian society. He could imagine that the official separation had already been released, and her friends were rallying to her side, now that she had dissociated herself from him.

But he preferred to remember her in that crimson gown, on that long-ago Festival night, looking up at him with love in her eyes. And the roar of approval when he had announced from the steps that Lycoris had agreed to marry him. Though they had spent only days out of the year together, their marriage was legendary. Collections of their letters had been released at their ten-year and twenty-year anniversaries. He could remember golden moments, precious and frozen in time forever because of his poetry. Outshining them all was the birth of his sons. He had not written a line since his youngest son had died at the hands of the Maquis—

"Oh, excuse me—"

Gul Evek looked around vaguely, still caught in the vivid past. A tall slender man in a red Starfleet uniform stood awkwardly in the aisle, having leaped down most of the steps.

"I'm sorry," the man said. "I didn't see you there. Didn't mean to startle you."

He came down the steps at a more reasonable pace, right to the window. "She's a beauty, your ship."

Gul Evek murmured, "Indeed she is."

The man gestured to himself, "I'm Tom Paris."

Evek would never have been approached this way by any of his subordinates. They would have first requested and received permission to speak. And they would only approach with good reason.

Evek looked at the young human male sharply. He was wearing a uniform, but it was stripped of rank and insignia.

"You aren't a crewmember of *Voyager*," Evek said flatly.

"It shows that much?" Paris asked.

"Yes."

Paris laughed shortly, but the humor had gone out of his voice. He sat down abruptly, no longer trying to engage Gul Evek in conversation.

For a long time they both simply stared at the passing starfield and the glow of the forcefield surrounding the *Vetar*.

Then Paris sighed. "I made a mistake. I didn't know it was going to ruin the rest of my life."

Evek had to laugh shortly at that. "I have had that experience."

"You have?"

"Yes. I had hoped to redeem myself." Evek thought about the past few weeks spent uselessly searching for the *Selva*, so he could place the blame where it properly belonged. Without Seska to stand trial, the prosecutor would focus on Evek's decision to authorize the ambush plan. "I had such hope . . ."

Paris was suddenly interested. "You weren't able to fix things? I've been wondering if it's possible . . ."

"No. My military career is over. There is nothing else." There was an awkward silence, then Evek stood up. "I will leave now."

Evek looked one more time at the *Vetar.* It had been magnificent while it lasted.

Then he turned his back on the past and walked up the stairs to face what would be expected of him.

Chapter Ten

PARIS SAT BACK down after the Cardassian had left the observation lounge. Their discussion seemed unfinished. It felt like they had just been getting to the crux of the matter when it had broken off.

He frowned at the *Vetar*. Why was it he could be so glib when it came to talking about nothing, but when the conversation suddenly got real, he let it slip away? He didn't even know who the Cardassian was, though he was obviously a senior officer of some sort.

After a while he started to get up, when his hand hit something on the cushion next to him. A small isolinear storage device was lying there. It was rounder than the usual type, and had a symbol on the casing. Paris recognized it as Cardassian.

It was near where the Cardassian had been sitting, so it must belong to him. Maybe he mistakenly dropped it.

Paris had to admit that his first impulse was to access its contents. But that could get him in more trouble than his curiosity was worth.

He could just give the rod to Captain Janeway to return to its proper owner . . . but he felt an empathy for the older man, and wanted to talk to the Cardassian some more.

He took the rod over to the wall screen that was tied into the ship's computers. Holding the rod up, Paris requested a diagram of Cardassian insignia. Comparing the rod to the computer drawings, he realized it matched the one reserved for Guls. Had he been talking to the commander of the Vetar?

"Computer, display image of the commander of the *Vetar*," Paris requested.

"Gul Aman Evek is currently in command of the Galor-*class warship* Vetar," the computer responded.

It was the same Cardassian. *Well, what do you know . . .* Paris thought, *even the big fish fry sometimes.*

Paris cleared the screen and briefly reconsidered giving the rod to Captain Janeway. But Alpha shift wouldn't start for hours. He didn't need to wake her for this.

The computer gave him the location of Gul Evek's quarters. Paris strolled quickly through the empty corridors. There was only a skeleton crew on duty. Everyone else was sleeping, after the exhausting evacuation.

Paris stood in front of Gul Evek's door, knowing the chime would ring on the inside. He also said, "Gul Evek, sir, I wanted to return your isolinear rod. You left it in the observation lounge."

He waited but there was no answer.

"Gul Evek? It's Tom Paris. We spoke in the observation lounge."

Still no answer. Paris asked, "Computer, is this Gul Evek's quarters?"

"*Affirmative.*"

"Where is he now?"

"*Gul Evek is in his quarters on deck 5.*"

So, maybe the gul was asleep, or didn't care about the rod, or didn't want to see anyone right now. Paris remembered feeling the same way on Caldik Prime, when he withdrew from everyone. But it had backfired when they thought he was being a snob, as if his father, the admiral, would get him off the charges. Paris had realized too late he was the only one who knew that his father wouldn't lift a finger to help him. His father believed he deserved his punishment.

Paris hesitated, only because Gul Evek had looked exhausted to the point of being ill. "Computer, is Gul Evek okay?"

"*Authorization for medical scan?*" the computer requested.

"Paris, Tom," he said, as he had been saying in sickbay whenever he had requested a scan. Dr. Bist must not have had time to rescind the authorization, because the computer immediately said, "*Medical scan underway.*"

Paris wondered if he hadn't made one of his patented idiotic mistakes. It could be considered invasive, what he had just done . . . But they were still under emergency status, and he had been assisting in sickbay all night. As far as he knew, Gul Evek hadn't received medical treatment yet.

"There are no life-signs present in Gul Evek's quarters," the computer reported.

"No life-signs . . . but you said he was in there. . . ." Then Paris realized what it meant.

"Computer, tell Captain Janeway—"

"Captain Janeway has been notified."

Paris leaned against the wall, waiting for everyone to arrive. This was the last thing he needed! Why hadn't he gone back to his quarters, even if he couldn't sleep? Why couldn't he keep his mouth shut? His trouble was that he talked too damn much.

Security was the first to arrive, and they treated him like a fugitive caught at the scene of a crime. One of them pushed him back when he tried to move away from the wall.

"Hey, I'm the guy who reported it," Paris reminded the officer.

"You stay right there," Rollins ordered as he arrived. He overrode the door control and went inside, with two other security guards following him. An ensign stayed outside with Paris.

Captain Janeway and Dr. Bist arrived as Rollins emerged. "Gul Evek is dead, Captain."

Janeway glanced at Paris, and he protested, "It's not my fault!"

"Come with me," she ordered, to his surprise. He followed her into Gul Evek's quarters.

It was dark inside, so she said, "Lights up."

"That's the way I found it," Rollins told her. "No signs of a struggle. He's in here."

Gul Evek was lying on his bed in his uniform, his arms down at his side. Paris almost didn't recognize him. He looked much older and smaller than he remembered. The man's force of personality, his commanding presence, had been deceiving.

"There lies a legend," Janeway murmured.

Dr. Bist finished scanning him. "Poisoned. The structure is identical with a common Cardassian poison. There's traces of it in his mouth."

"What a terrible way for the soldier-bard to die," Janeway said. Then she turned to Paris. "What do you know about this?"

"We were talking in the observation lounge." Paris held out the isolinear rod to Janeway. "He left this behind by accident, I think. I was trying to return it to him. When he didn't answer the door. . . ."

Janeway took the storage device, recognizing the Cardassian command insignia.

Dr. Bist packed up his tricorder. "So you're planning on entering the medical field, Mister Paris? I wouldn't count on it, if I were you. Leave the medical scans to me from now on."

"Yes, sir," Paris said evenly. Sarcasm he could handle. He was just glad when Janeway didn't add her own disapproval.

"Did you have any indication he was going to do this?" Janeway asked.

"He said his military career was over," Paris admitted. "But I never thought this would happen. I mean, I lost everything—a couple of times—and I know you're supposed to keep on trying."

Janeway gave him a harder look. "I think you've got the right idea, Mister Paris. Keep on trying." She actually patted him on the shoulder. "You're dismissed. Try to get a couple of hours sleep. We'll need you in the morning."

"Aye, Captain," he said, feeling a little better.

Janeway took the isolinear rod up to her ready room, knowing she would have to notify Gul Dukat on the *Prakesh* that Gul Evek was dead. But the rod was a problem. After a moment's consideration, she placed it into the computer slot.

A striking Cardassian woman appeared on the screen. "I cannot live this way any longer, Aman Evek. We are disgraced and the outrage on Prime over Opek Nor continues. I cannot save myself as well as you. So I must save myself. I have begun proceedings to separate—"

Janeway cut off the message when it was clear it was personal. It certainly helped to explain Gul Evek's suicide. Tragic. He could have retired out of the public eye and written beautifully about survival and rebirth. Instead, he had ended it, ending all of his other options.

She ordered ops to open a channel to the *Prakesh*. When Gul Dukat finally came on the viewscreen, she told him, "I'm sorry to inform you, but Gul Evek is dead. Our doctor says it was poison, self-inflicted."

Janeway expected some sort of suspicious reaction. She would seriously question any Cardassian commander who claimed a Starfleet captain had died in custody.

But Gul Dukat didn't seem surprised, or even very concerned. "Very well. We will intercept shortly. Prepare the *Vetar*'s crew for transfer."

"Acknowledged." She lifted the isolinear rod. "Gul Evek left behind this. It appears to be a message from a woman, I believe it is his . . . mate."

"Lycoris?" Dukat hesitated. "Do Gul Evek a favor, Captain. Destroy it. There is no need to further tarnish the commander's name."

Janeway acknowledged, uncomfortable with the curt way Dukat ended the transmission.

Next she notified Evek's first officer, Belak. He, too, did not seem surprised to hear the news that Aman Evek was dead. Janeway ended up shaking her head, faced with the fact that there was a great deal that Starfleet didn't understand about the Cardassians.

She checked the reports that had been filed, and saw that Gul Evek had sent her the information she had requested. She sat down with a cup of hot coffee and began scanning through the data. The trajectory and coordinates of the *Selva* when she was last seen by the *Vetar* were included. That was where *Voyager* would start looking for the Maquis ship.

She read through the rest of the entries, and was particularly intrigued by the last logs, describing what had happened after the subspace shockwave hit the *Vetar*. Gul Evek said the very air glowed from luminescence as the molecules in their moisture-rich atmosphere underwent dissociation.

Janeway had read the report on the Badlands anomaly submitted several years ago by Commander Data. He had suggested several intriguing theories as to what was causing the phenomenon. The intense gravitational power of the plasma storms was one option, yet how could it rip open subspace and produce periodic, seemingly random shockwaves containing tetryon particles?

"Computer, give me a schematic of the Badlands sector," she ordered.

A starmap appeared on the monitor. The plasma storms were marked in elliptical overlapping shadows filling over a quarter of the sector.

"Indicate the location of previous ships that have encountered the Badlands anomaly."

Voyager, Enterprise, Enterprise-D, and several other vessels appeared on the screen. Janeway saw that one of them was the *Vetar*. At the bottom were listed reports of Maquis ships rumored to have encountered the anomaly; however, exact coordinates were unknown.

Janeway entered the coordinates of the *Selva* according to Gul Evek's report, and another tiny ship appeared, much further away than the others.

There was one ship she didn't recognize at first. On magnifying, she read it was a Romulan bird-of-prey: the unnamed vessel had exploded at approximately the same time the nearby *Enterprise* was hit by a shockwave.

"Computer, estimate each vessel's range from the Badlands anomaly, according to the duration of the gravity loss."

A shaded buffer zone appeared around each of the

dots reaching at its furthest extent, with *Voyager,* to 200 million kilometers.

There was a vague pattern, as some segments of the buffer zones lined up between the dots. "Add trajectory indicators," Janeway ordered.

The ships had been going in various directions when they encountered the phenomenon. But the dotted line indicator for the Romulan bird-of-prey caught her attention. It was aimed directly up one side of the Badlands, into the region where the *Enterprise* had encountered the anomaly. If she extended the trajectory line, it pointed at the tiny Maquis ship, the *Selva,* which was almost as far away from the Badlands on one side as *Voyager* had been on the other.

The vague pattern of dots was suddenly looking like the sketch of an orbital trajectory. Starting with the Romulan bird-of-prey.

Captain Kirk of the starship *Enterprise* had theorized that the anomaly was caused by a Romulan booby trap. But the Starfleet science ships that had investigated the Badlands over the intervening decades had assumed that the Romulan warbird was destroyed by the same shockwave that had damaged the *Enterprise.*

But what if Kirk had been right all along, and the warbird *was* responsible for the Badlands anomaly?

That's when it all came together. Tetryons were caused by subspace rifts. A year after the *Enterprise*-D had encountered the anomaly, they had discovered that Romulan warbirds were powered by artificial quantum singularities. An AQS was in essence a microscopic black hole. Once they were enabled, they could not be deactivated.

Janeway looked at the schematic again. What if that Romulan bird-of-prey of a hundred years ago had contained a prototype AQS power source? What if the ship had been destroyed, and the AQS escaped its containment field? What if it was still out here, caught in orbit around the plasma-heavy Badlands?

"My God," she softly exclaimed. "It's a free-range AQS."

No wonder they couldn't find the source of the tetryon shockwaves. The AQS must be moving much faster than the speed of light, at nearly warp 10. It would be impossible for sensors to detect until it was on top of them and already gone in its tremendous orbit. The subspace shockwave would therefore dissipate quickly, less than two hundred million kilometers away from the source. Any ships unlucky enough to be close to it when it passed by would suffer a lapse in gravity, sensor overload, and disruption of the power circuits. And the passage of tetryons through the ship would cause radiation poisoning in the crew members.

"Captain," Cavit called from the bridge. "The Prakesh is approaching."

"Standard procedure," she ordered Cavit. No use taking any chances now.

Quickly she downloaded the data she had obtained from Gul Evek and initiated an encoded transmission to Starfleet Headquarters. She included her own schematic of the Badlands and a summary of her theory that a "free-range" AQS was currently in a long elliptical orbit around the Badlands plasma storms.

Janeway sent the secured transmission to Starfleet, then set her empty cup down on the replicator. It was an early start to the day, but at least something positive might result from the *Vetar*'s encounter with the AQS.

She paused before stepping onto the bridge. The utter waste of Aman Evek's death was difficult for her to grasp. The last lines of his *Long Voyage to Hutet* kept echoing in her head:

> There never was a war that was not inward,
> Never a heart conquered from without.
> What is our innocence, where is our guilt?
> Where is the courage for the unanswered question
> That in misfortune, even in death,
> Can defeat our mortality?

Chapter Eleven

KIM WAS AWAKENED by the general announcement that the transfer of *Vetar* crewmembers would begin shortly. Since he had worked an extra half-shift during the evacuation, he hadn't been called to assist. But he couldn't go back to sleep, and Alpha shift would start soon, so he went ahead and got dressed.

This time, he left the holodisc by his bedside. He didn't need to activate it to see Libby's smile. He had told her that serving on *Voyager* was important for his career. She hadn't been able to hide her disappointment that he would be gone on missions for months at a time.

But even if they were married, *Voyager* was not the type of starship that could accommodate family members. After only one day on duty, Kim could appreciate why.

He walked out of his quarters right into a long line of Cardassians heading to the transporter rooms on deck 4.

"Hey, mate," called an engineering technician. "Give us a hand here."

Kim helped support a Cardassian woman who was having trouble walking. "You can lean on me," he told her.

She could only grunt in thanks, as she took his arm. Her teeth were bared and she was breathing heavily. When she stumbled, Kim had to catch her around the waist to keep her from falling. He was surprised at how strong and solid the Cardassian felt, yet she could hardly hold herself up.

There was a line outside of transporter room one, so Kim helped her lean against a wall. She seemed more comfortable when he wasn't touching her.

Tom Paris came over with a medical regenerator. "You look like you're in some distress." He slowly passed the regenerator in front of her body. "That should help relieve the pain."

After Paris had finished and moved on, Kim passed off the Cardassian crewmember to the team assisting inside the transporter room. He ran to catch up with Paris.

Another line of Cardassians was approaching. They backed into a doorway to let them pass, then Tom sighed and followed them back to the transporter room.

"It's eerie," Kim whispered. "I don't think I've heard one of them speak. Their ship isn't that badly damaged—"

Paris stopped before they reached the line of Cardassians waiting outside the transporter room. "Gul Evek committed suicide last night."

"What?!" Kim glanced toward the Cardassians. He lowered his voice. "Why?"

Paris looked upset. "From what they've said, I think they expected him to do it."

"Why . . . ?" Kim repeated, unable to comprehend such a thing.

"Gul Evek said his military career was over."

Kim blinked. "That's not any reason to kill yourself! He was a great writer—that's what Captain Janeway said last night."

Paris shrugged. "It's not easy to lose everything. Sometimes you just want to give up trying."

"I never imagined . . ." *It would be like this,* he finished silently.

Paris began regenerating the Cardassian at the end of the line. Kim thought Paris's expression was almost as bleak as the Cardassian's.

"Can I help you do that?" Kim offered to Paris.

But Lieutenant Commander Cavit was walking down the line of waiting Cardassians, watching them even more closely than the security volunteers. He heard Kim, and gave Paris a dismissive glance, cutting between the two men.

"You should get something to eat before reporting to the bridge, Ensign," Cavit told him. "I'm going up to the mess hall myself. Come on."

Kim gave Paris a startled look. But Paris turned away and methodically began passing the regenerator over the Cardassian.

"See you around," Kim told Paris.

Paris lifted one hand, but didn't pause in his work.

Kim left with Lieutenant Commander Cavit, as his suggestion had had the tone of an order. First Dr. Bist had been rude to Tom Paris, and now Lieutenant Commander Cavit. Kim didn't understand why, but it didn't seem fair. Paris may just be an "observer," but he was assigned to *Voyager* and should be treated with respect.

And as far as Kim could tell, Paris was working hard, being helpful and nice to everyone. Kim would never forget how Paris had turned his first encounter with a Ferengi from a near-disaster into a shared laugh. He wondered how much latinum that Ferengi would have gotten off him if Paris hadn't told him those Lobi crystals were worthless.

Kim decided he was going to find out once and for all what was going on with Tom Paris.

Paris kept giving cellular regeneration treatments until there were no more Cardassians on board *Voyager*. He kept thinking of what the EMH had said about the lack of medical attention in Cardassia. This could be the last treatment some of them received.

He was exhausted, but when he was done he went to the observation lounge where he had met Gul Evek. There, he watched the *Prakesh* take the *Vetar* in tow. The two ships curved away from *Voyager,* and quickly grew smaller. Then there was the brief spatial distortion of the starfield as they entered warp.

So . . . it was over. He could give up, like Gul Evek, or keep on trying.

Whistling, he put his hands in his pockets and headed up to the officer's mess hall on deck 2. He hesitated outside the door, but decided he had nothing to lose.

The first thing he saw when he went inside was Ensign Kim sitting with Dr. Bist and First Officer Cavit. The three of them looked over, and Paris instantly knew they had been talking about him.

He went to the replicator controls, trying frantically to think of something to order before they kicked him out. He had known that Kim would find out about him sooner or later, but it wasn't a pleasant feeling to lose someone's respect. Even a baby ensign's.

"Tomato soup," he said, choosing one of his favorites at random.

"There are fourteen varieties of tomato soup available from this replicator. With rice. With vegetables. Bolian-style . . ."

"Plain," he said flatly.

"Specify hot or chilled."

"Hot. Hot . . . plain . . . tomato soup." Paris wanted to kick the wall to make the thing work. He just wished everyone would stop staring at him.

The replicator whirred and a bowl of soup appeared. Paris placed it on his tray and turned.

Dr. Bist and Lieutenant Commander Cavit were leaving. Neither deigned to glance his way. Ensign Kim was still sitting at the table, gazing down at his food, obviously aware that Paris was standing there like an idiot looking at him.

Paris figured once again that he had nothing to lose. At least he hadn't been tossed out of the officer's mess.

He sat down across from Kim, affecting false cheer. "There, you see, I told you it wouldn't take long."

Kim was more serious than Paris had ever seen him. "Is it true?" he asked.

"Was the accident my fault? Yes. Pilot error. But it took a while to admit it." He took a sip of soup, but had difficulty swallowing. "Fourteen varieties and they can't even get plain tomato soup right. . . ."

"They said you falsified reports," Kim said accusingly.

"That's right."

"Why?" Kim asked, as if unable to believe it was true even when Paris admitted it.

"What's the difference? I lied." This was harder than he thought it would be.

"But then you came forward and admitted it was your fault."

Paris sighed. There was no way around it. "I'll tell you the truth, Harry. All I had to do was keep my mouth shut and I was home free. But I couldn't. The ghosts of those three dead officers came to me in the middle of the night . . . so I confessed." He shook his head. "Worst mistake I ever made. But not the last. After they cashiered me out of Starfleet, I went looking for a fight and I found the Maquis. On my *first* assignment I was caught."

Kim hesitated. "Must have been especially tough for you, being the son of an admiral."

"Frankly, I think it was tougher on my father than it

was on me." Paris stood up to throw away his soup. He liked this Harry Kim fellow, so he said, "Look, I know those guys told you to stay away from me, and you know what? You ought to listen to them. I'm not exactly a good-luck charm."

Kim stood up too. "I don't need anyone to choose my friends for me."

Paris hadn't expected that, and he smiled at Kim. He didn't know what to say.

"Janeway to Paris," Janeway said over the com.

"Go ahead," Paris replied.

"Report to the bridge. We're approaching the Badlands."

Captain Janeway watched the viewscreen as they entered the plasma storms of the Badlands. The vibrant gold plasma flares were muted by the viewscreen damping system, but their power was evident.

The ship shuddered, but Janeway was pleased the inertial dampers were working so well. Utopia Planetia certainly knew what they were doing when they had built this ship. Stadi seemed exhilarated, flying *Voyager* around the dangerous funnel-like flares.

Janeway went to the security station to look over the shoulder of Ensign Rollins with Cavit standing next to her. They both noticed that Ensign Kim and Tom Paris had entered the bridge together. Cavit made a small disapproving sound under his breath, but Janeway was glad to see the two side-by-side. Paris could only benefit from being around someone like Kim. She intended to remind Cavit of that later.

Janeway gestured to the schematic of the Badlands on the security screen. It was magnified, revealing the area surrounding the coordinates where the Maquis ship had last been seen by the *Vetar*.

She explained to Paris, "The Cardassians gave us the last known heading of the Maquis ship. And we have charts of plasma-storm activity for the day it disappeared. With a little help, we might be able to approximate its course."

Paris moved closer to study the schematic. Janeway couldn't tell if he felt a twinge of regret at betraying the Maquis. "I'd guess they were trying to get to one of the Class-M planetoids in the Terikof Belt."

Cavit leaned over Rollins to point to the schematic. "That would take them here."

Rollins input the information and an overlay of plasma activity covered the schematic with concentric rings. "The plasma storms would have forced them in this direction."

"Adjust our course to match."

"Aye, Captain," Cavit replied. He went forward to speak to Stadi at the conn. Janeway walked back to her command chair. With nothing else to do, Paris followed her.

Janeway realized Paris had not been briefed along with the rest of the bridge crew. "The Cardassians claim they forced the Maquis ship into a plasma storm, where it was destroyed. But our probes haven't picked up any debris."

"A plasma storm might not leave any debris," Paris pointed out.

"We'd still be able to pick up a resonance trace from the warp core—"

Ensign Kim suddenly said, "Captain, I'm reading a coherent tetryon beam scanning us."

Scanning? "Origin, Mister Kim?"

Kim was working on the ops panel. "I'm not sure." He hesitated, clearly trying to find out more. "There's also a displacement wave moving toward us."

"On screen," Janeway ordered.

A huge subspace wave was deforming the plasma, sweeping across the Badlands toward them. The fact that they could see it meant it was moving too slowly to be the subspace shockwave which had struck down the *Vetar.*

"Analysis," Janeway said.

"Some kind of polarized magnetic variation," Kim said vaguely.

Cavit turned to her. "We might be able to disperse it with a graviton particle field."

"Do it," Janeway ordered.

Cavit moved to the tactical station, replacing the officer there. Janeway knew tetryons were dangerous simply because they indicated the presence of a subspace intrusion on real space-time. A graviton particle field should reimpose a gravitational constant on the area. "Red alert." Janeway told Stadi, "Move us away from it, Lieutenant."

"New heading four-one-zero mark one-eight."

"Initiating graviton field," Cavit reported.

The wave grew larger, moving even faster. Janeway

glanced back as Kim reacted. "The graviton field had no effect!"

"Full impulse," she ordered.

The light on the viewscreen was brighter now, as plasma around them reacted to the subspace distortion.

"The wave will intercept us in twenty seconds," Kim announced.

"Can we go to warp?" Janeway asked, raising her voice as the ship shook harder.

Stadi said, "Not until we clear the plasma field, Captain."

"Eight seconds," Kim warned.

"Brace for impact," Janeway ordered.

"Three . . . ," Kim said.

Janeway gripped the chair as *Voyager* was lifted up, tossed as if there were no such thing as inertial dampers. She went flying, as everything turned bright white—weightless, formless, no sound, no sight, only a ringing in her ears and her heartbeat.

In the Badlands, the plasma flares wheeled and bulged, turning from white to flaming orange again. *Voyager* was gone.

PART 4

STAR TREK
DEEP SPACE NINE°

Stardate 50502.4
Year 2373

Just prior to the Dominion War

PART 4

Chapter One

CAPTAIN BENJAMIN SISKO stood at the railing overlooking the hangar bay of the former Maquis base. It had long been hidden on a Class-M asteroid in the Terikof Belt, until Starfleet had discovered its location. Above him was the large oval of the hangar door, with the rest of the complex cleverly concealed inside the bored-out rock of the extinct volcano.

The forcefield was transparent blue, allowing Sisko to see beyond the thin atmospheric layer to the glinting asteroids that filled the Terikof Belt. The Badlands were a ruddy smear across the lower portion of the hangar door.

Both Starfleet and the Cardassians had looked long and hard for this elusive base. For too long, after the Klingons had attacked the Cardassian Empire and destroyed their fleet, the Maquis had been running free in

133

the Badlands sector. The Maquis had escalated their territorial war, and might have won if they hadn't lost their strongest leader, Michael Eddington. But now Starfleet had the Maquis on the run.

Lieutenant Commander Worf approached Sisko and stood at attention. "Sir, the last of the captured Maquis have been beamed aboard the transports."

"Thank you, Worf." Sisko noticed that Worf's gray uniform was smudged, as if the Klingon had been helping to load cargo onto the transport platforms. "I'll return to the *Defiant* shortly."

Worf was too stoic to show his surprise, but Sisko knew why the Klingon hesitated. Their job was done. Their orders were to return to DS9 while the Starfleet vessels, the *Northstar* and the *Lakota*, escorted the Maquis transports to their new colony worlds. They would return in the next few weeks to patrol the Badlands for Maquis stragglers. Most of the Maquis had already fled the Badlands sector, but there were still strong pockets of resistance along the Cardassian border.

"Dismissed," Sisko told Worf.

The captain headed down to the floor of the hangar bay, empty now of everything but crates and debris. The massive computer used to calculate the trajectory of asteroids in the Terikof Belt had been carefully removed and placed on the *Northstar.* It would now be used for weather control for the new Maquis colony on Pelosis 3.

Sisko wanted to savor this moment, when the thorn of the Maquis had at last been removed from his side.

He heard the high-pitched whine of a transporter as Worf beamed off the abandoned base, and he curled his hand into a fist. "Yes!"

Sisko had finally beaten Michael Eddington, his former security officer on DS9. When Eddington surrendered, he had pulled the spine from the Maquis resistance. After that it had taken remarkably little— promises of amnesty and resettlement—for the captured Maquis to reveal their hidden bases. Sisko believed they were all tired of the fighting and wanted to get on with their lives.

Sisko would never forget Eddington's expression when he realized that his capture was resulting in the end of the dreams of the Maquis. It was a little reality seeping into his grand illusion of living out *Les Misérables*.

And now it was done. For several years the Maquis had interfered with shipping and attacked Cardassian colonies along the border. They had killed many people, both Federation and Cardassian citizens. The only good thing that had come from the conflict, as far as Sisko could tell, was the common ground it had given the Federation and the Cardassian Empire. The two very different humanoid types were finally cooperating after generations of war.

As he walked among the debris, noting the plasma burns on the well-used hangar floor, Sisko knew he had never really hated the Maquis. He had received dozens of congratulatory messages from Starfleet officers who had fought against the Maquis, some of whom would never forgive the rebels. But not Sisko.

At one time, Sisko thought it was Eddington's betrayal that he could not live with. Eddington had been a Starfleet officer, yet he dishonored his commission and had deceived everyone on DS9 for over a year.

But Kasidy had also been working for the Maquis when Sisko fell in love with her. She had deceived him while smuggling weapons to the Maquis. It had been a shock when she was caught and had to serve six months in prison. Yet Sisko felt no reservations about accepting Kasidy back into his heart

At this moment of victory, which felt oddly hollow, Sisko realized his zeal in the past few weeks for tracking down and bringing Eddington to justice had been covering a deeper obsession. Nothing had been the same since the Prophets had sent him the visions of B'hala.

The Prophets had touched him and shown him nonlinear time. He had been able to see the past and the future like some great pattern that made perfect sense. But Dr. Bashir had reversed the effects, taking it away too soon.

Sisko had almost understood everything, standing on the cusp of time, seeing it all at once. He had seen enough to know that Bajor must wait to join the Federation. Somehow, it was important both to their survival and to the survival of the Alpha Quadrant. He had been willing to lose his Starfleet commission if it came to that, but he had to speak the truth.

Now he could see that his pursuit of Eddington and the Maquis wasn't about what *they* had done. It was about proving *himself* to Starfleet—proving he was in control of the situation.

Because deep down, Sisko knew he wasn't in control. His visions had shown him chaos bearing down on the Alpha Quadrant. Starfleet was under the illusion that the region was finally stabilized. Certainly their situation had improved since they had discovered that General Martok was a changeling and the Klingons had joined forces with the Federation again. The Cardassians were even cooperating with defense strategies. The Alpha Quadrant finally seemed to be united in the face of the threat from the Dominion.

Sisko hit his comm badge. "One to beam up."

His last view of the legendary Maquis base was one of desolation and empty dreams.

On the *Defiant*, Sisko immediately took the command seat from Worf. Lieutenant Commander Dax was at the helm, as usual, but many of the other stations were staffed by secondary personnel. Chief O'Brien and Major Kira had chosen to remain on DS9, tending to the O'Briens' week-old baby, Kirayoshi.

"Is the containment generator ready?" Sisko asked.

"Aye, Captain," Worf acknowledged.

"Activate it." Sisko pressed the tips of his fingers together under his chin, watching as the blue glow of the hangar forcefield slowly darkened. Soon there was blackness, with nothing to show the entrance into the volcano. The machinery operating the containment field was located inside the base. The only way to drop the field was by issuing the proper safety codes. That would help prevent stray Maquis from trying to reestablish their stronghold in the Badlands sector.

"Containment field activated and secure," Worf reported. "We are being hailed by the *Northstar.*"

Captain Mikhail appeared on the viewscreen, his dark eyes gleaming with satisfaction. "So it's done, Captain Sisko. We'll be on our way."

"See you back at DS9 in a few weeks," Sisko told Mikhail.

"Always a pleasure." With a flash of white teeth beneath his black mustache, Mikhail signed off.

"The Starfleet transports are leaving orbit," Dax announced, as the *Northstar* and the *Lakota* departed with their sometime-Maquis colonists.

"Set course for DS9," Sisko ordered. "When we clear the sensor shadow, go to warp 7."

He hardly noticed the satisfied murmurs as the crew turned their vessel for home. Now that the Maquis weren't sitting at their backs taking potshots at both the Federation and Cardassia, they had every reason to believe that things would improve.

But Sisko knew better. He was the one sitting in the doorway, able to see the hoards as they approached. The responsibility for stopping them lay on his shoulders, and his people would be the first to die if—*when*—something went wrong.

Chapter Two

ODO SIGNED the padd listing the names of the last of the Maquis leaders that DS9 had been holding in their brig. Captain Sanders watched as his security officers beamed back to the *Malinche* with the Maquis.

"So, that's the end to that," Sanders said with great satisfaction.

Odo handed him the padd. "You have a long journey back to Earth."

"I volunteered for this duty," Captain Sanders replied. "We've waited a long time to see the collapse of the Maquis."

Odo made a polite sound of agreement. The Maquis had benefited from the experience some of their leaders had gained during the Bajoran resistance to the Cardassian Occupation. They also had benefited from the knowledge of Starfleet officers who had resigned their commission to fight against the Federation-Cardassian treaty. The Maquis had been a formidable enemy, and it had taken the combined forces of Starfleet and Cardassia to stop them.

Odo still had trouble believing that the Cardassians were cooperating with Starfleet and the Bajoran government. After spending many years working under the Cardassians, he thought it didn't fit his expectations of them. But who was he to question Starfleet? Sometimes he felt lucky that they let a changeling continue as security chief of DS9. But after Odo had uncovered Eddington's deception, they would have a difficult time doubting *him*.

With a cheery wave, Captain Sanders transported out of the security office.

And Odo was done. Not just for the day, but done with the problem of the Maquis. He knew that if he were human, he would be celebrating right now along with everyone else in Quark's bar.

But the first and last time Odo had celebrated in Quark's had been a week before, with Dr. Mora Pol, his surrogate father. Later that night, the baby changeling had suddenly died.

Odo had bought the baby changeling from Quark for eight slips of latinum, knowing instantly by the color that it was sick. Dr. Bashir determined it had been exposed to a massive amount of tetryon radiation. Though they had purged the isotopes, its morphogenic matrix had destabalized. The radiation had irrevocably damaged its cytoplasm. It died in his hand.

Odo looked down at his hand. The baby changeling

had been absorbed by his skin, and in dying had integrated itself with Odo's body, given him back his shapeshifting ability.

He could hear Dr. Mora Pol saying right before he left for Bajor, "Think of it as a gift. Something the little changeling wanted you to have."

Odo had been telling himself that for days, but it wasn't enough. The experience had been too precious and exhilarating. He had been distracting himself with other work, only allowing himself to feel the loss when he was alone in his quarters where he could revert to his gelatinous state.

During the guard shift change, the muted sound of voices drifted inside his office. Everyone was at Quark's bar, celebrating their victory over the Maquis.

He couldn't remember the last time he had felt so alone.

Odo passed command of security to his lieutenant and left the office. He hesitated outside, but instead of returning to his quarters, he headed directly to Quark's.

The Promenade echoed with the sound of people talking and laughing. The smell from the Klingon restaurant was particularly noxious today. It blended unpleasantly with the incense burned outside the Bajoran temple.

Inside Quark's, Leeta gleefully cried out, "Dabo!" The gaming table was surrounded by avid players.

Odo paused in the doorway, looking for Quark. The Ferengi wasn't in the Dabo crowd, where stakes were obviously high. He also wasn't at the bar, where two new barmaids were swamped with customers.

Odo sighed and dived into the merry throng. He spotted Chief O'Brien and Dr. Bashir sitting at a table, unable to play darts because of the number of people in the bar. As he got closer, Odo realized Kira was with them. Kira had been spending a great deal of time with the O'Briens, even after Kirayoshi was born. Odo thought Kira's expression was wistful despite the revelry going on around her. She missed her baby as much as he missed his.

O'Brien saw Odo and waved for him to join them. But now that Odo had made up his mind, he didn't want to delay any longer. He stiffly nodded back and continued looking for Quark.

He found the Ferengi on the mezzanine leading to the holosuites. Two Caldonians and an Andorian were arguing about whose turn it was to use the holosuite. Quark was trying to jack up the price while pretending to mediate.

Odo didn't intend to wait for the bidding war to end. "Quark, I have to talk—"

"Sorry, Odo," Quark interrupted, raising a skinny hand. "I've already told Bashir and O'Brien that I don't have a holosuite available for them tonight." He gestured at the overflowing bar. "Repeat customers are one thing, but I'm getting top latinum for these 'suites tonight." Turning to the others, Quark added, "And I mean *lots* of strips."

"Quark . . . ," Odo said warningly. "This won't take long."

Quark was still smiling but he made an exasperated sound at being pulled away from a deal in the works.

He followed Odo impatiently to the other end of the mezzanine. "Whatever it is, I haven't done anything—"

"Oh, shut up and listen to me," Odo told him. "I need to know where you got that baby changeling."

Quark pulled himself up to his full height. *"That's why you interrupted a business deal? Rule of Acquisition No. 30: A wise man knows that confidentiality equals profit."*

"I don't *care* about profit," Odo told him. "I want to know where that changeling came from. How did it get exposed to tetryon radiation? Consider this an investigation of the crime of murder." Odo leaned in closer when he realized that Quark's attention was wandering back to his impatient holosuite customers. "Maybe *you* exposed it to tetryon radiation. . . ."

"Me?" Typical. Quark feigned innocence even when he was innocent. "Where would I get tetryon radiation?"

"That's what I'd like to know."

Quark hesitated, then he realized he was losing the interest of his holosuite patrons. One of the Caldonians was pointing down at the Dabo table, arguing with her companion.

"All right, since it doesn't matter anyway," Quark said. "I got it from a Maquis smuggler. He would stop in every once in a while, but now I guess Starfleet's got him."

"Who is it?" Odo wished he had asked Quark yesterday. What if it was one of the men who had been in his brig, the ones who were just taken by the *Malinche?*

"Only name I knew him by was Hab." Quark started back to his customers. "That's all I can tell you."

Odo let Quark go, thinking quickly. Hab. That didn't match any of the names he had seen on the lists of Maquis detainees or colonists. He had never heard of Hab, the smuggler.

But there was somebody on DS9 who might know a Maquis smuggler named Hab. That was Captain Kasidy Yates.

Captain Yates had returned to the station six weeks ago and immediately resumed her former job with the Bajoran Ministry of Commerce. Odo was certain that Sisko's role as the Emissary to the Prophets had influenced her good fortune.

Odo scanned the bar looking for Captain Yates. Since she had once been a part of the Maquis, he didn't really expect to see her here. He hardly paused to acknowledge the occasional celebratory greeting as he pushed through the bar.

Odo hit his combadge and asked for the current location of Kasidy Yates.

As Odo hurried to Captain Yates's quarters on the habitat ring, he couldn't help remembering how he used to travel through DS9 before it was discovered that changelings were the dreaded Dominion. Before that, he had often shape-shifted through the grates and slipped through the conduits of the station. Now the sections were sealed from one another to prevent infiltrating changelings from having the run of DS9.

However, Odo was fairly positive that there were changelings on DS9. His people were too smart not to keep watch on the Starfleet base closest to the Gamma Quadrant. But vigilant blood checks had failed to uncover any Dominion spies.

When Odo reached Captain Yates's quarters, he hardly paused before hitting the door comm. He felt very unlike himself. Usually every move was well thought out and considered from every angle. But the baby changeling had altered his perspective. He had a strange compulsion to find out where it came from.

"Captain Yates, it's Odo," he said into the intercom.

After a long pause, the door opened to reveal Captain Yates. She was wearing a practical pilot's jumper, with her hair twisted into a secure knot. "Yes, can I help you, Constable?"

"Ah, yes," Odo repeated, suddenly at a loss for how to start. "I'm trying to find a smuggler called Hab. He sold Quark a baby changeling that was poisoned by tetryon radiation. I thought you might know him."

Yates crossed her arms. "What makes you think I would know?"

"He was working for the Maquis out of DS9. I thought, since you were part of the Maquis, too . . ."

"I served my time, and I didn't go back to the Maquis."

"I'm not accusing you of anything." Odo realized he couldn't pressure Captain Yates with threats of a murder investigation, like he'd done with Quark. He had nothing left but the truth. "This is a personal request."

"Personal?" she drawled, her arms still crossed. "You've barely acknowledged my return, Constable.

I'm not blind. I know you don't think I'm good enough for Benjamin."

Odo felt everything slipping away. He wanted desperately to mumble something and run away. But he forced himself to stay.

"Forgive me, Captain Yates," he said in a low voice. "It's not you. I'm that way with everyone." Suddenly it wasn't so hard to admit it. "But the baby changeling was different. Have you ever had children?"

"No," she replied, caught off guard. Her eyes shifted, and he wondered if she was thinking about Jake.

"That baby changeling made everything different for me," Odo explained. "I have to know what happened to it. Where it came from. Maybe there are others. . . ."

Her expression finally softened. "I'll see what I can do, Constable."

Odo awkwardly pulled back, nodding to the captain. All of his experience in investigating crimes threatened to go out the airlock with his newfound sense of urgency. He wanted to know everything *now*—but he knew he would have to wait.

Odo was in his gelatinous state, slowly rolling over the twisted arches of the jungle gym he had set up in his quarters. He had missed doing this when his people had forced him to remain solid as penance for killing a fellow shape-shifter. But that had been an accident. All along Odo felt as if they were really punishing him for staying with the solids instead of returning to the Great Link.

The computer interrupted him as he was rounding a

particularly tricky corner. *"Incoming message from Captain Kasidy Yates."*

Odo's mouth formed first, saying, "Yes! On the monitor."

"Odo?" Yates asked, unable to see him. "I know it's late . . . but I thought you would like to know what I found out."

Odo reformed into his Bajoran uniform before rushing to the monitor. "Yes? What is it?"

Captain Yates gave him a long look. "You had better not use this information against me . . ."

"Never!" he instantly agreed. "This is strictly personal. Now, please, tell me what you know."

She raised one brow at his insistence. "The baby was found adrift in the Badlands sector, near the Terikof Belt, by the same smuggler who sold it to Quark. He thought it was a dead changeling."

"Did you get the coordinates?" Odo asked.

"That's all I know," Kasidy said.

"Oh . . ."

"Do you know how difficult it was to find out that much?" Kasidy asked him. "The Maquis have scattered, Odo. Their network is broken. I had to call in a lot of favors just to get that much—"

"Thank you, Captain Yates," Odo said hastily. "I didn't mean to sound ungrateful. I'm just surprised that it was found in the Badlands. I wonder how it got there?"

"Well, at least that explains the tetryon poisoning," Kasidy told him.

Odo shook his head. "Excuse me?"

"You said it was sick because of tetryon radiation." She realized he didn't understand. "Haven't you heard of the Badlands anomaly? The Maquis called it the Badlands curse."

"Ah, yes . . . ," Odo said slowly, remembering now. "I have heard something about it. Starship crews were exposed to tetryon radiation."

"Ask anyone in the Maquis, they could tell you about the curse. The shockwave destroys warp drives and circuitry and makes everyone sick. Before you know it's there, it's gone. I've heard rumors the past year that it's caused by something that's orbiting the Badlands. But there's no way to know where it is or when it's coming."

"But if it passed near the baby changeling . . ." Odo said slowly.

"It would have been irradiated, poor thing," Kasidy said sadly. "I had a friend who nearly died from the Badlands curse. Somebody should do something about it."

"Yes, they should." Odo was already thinking of the ramifications. The Badlands sector lay adjacent to the Bajoran sector. Any changeling coming from that direction trying to get to the wormhole, lured home to the Gamma Quadrant as changelings were genetically programmed to do, would run the risk of exposure to deadly tetryon radiation. It could happen all over again . . . another baby changeling could die.

"Yes, we *should* do something," Odo said stronger. "Thank you, Captain Yates. I appreciate your efforts."

"Thank you, Odo." She winked at him. "And you can call me Kasidy from now on."

He hesitated. "Thank you, Kasidy. If there is anything I can do for you . . ." He didn't know what to say.

"Don't mention it, Odo."

After she signed off, Odo sat at his terminal considering the problem. It would not be easy, but somehow there must be a way to keep this from happening again.

Many light-years away, Romulan Centurion Seylok leaned back in his commander's chair. He was still not quite accustomed to the thought that the *Bokra* was his. She was the newest scout ship in the Romulan Star Empire. She had both speed and weapons, and they were at his command.

"Centurion!" Sublieutenant Retal announced, standing at attention.

Seylok could hear the subtle sneer in her tone, as if Sublieutenant Retal also couldn't believe that he was in command. Seylok had served under Retal several years ago. The entire crew knew Seylok had been a sublieutenant until last quarter, when he had been abruptly raised to the rank of centurion.

"Yes, sublieutenant?" he asked.

"We are entering the Alpha Quadrant," Retal informed him, her eyes not quite meeting his as per protocol.

"Stay on course," Seylok ordered. Retal saluted and turned smartly. She was a career military officer, while Seylok . . . The crew must suspect his sudden rise in the military ranks was because he was an agent of the Tal Shiar.

Seylok did not mind their whispers. He knew the work it had taken for him to get here. That, and the fortune brought to some in the midst of the great tragedy. Seylok had been a sublieutenant until many of the top Tal Shiar had been killed in the joint Romulan/Cardassian attack on the homeworld of the Dominion.

Now it was up to Centurion Seylok to end the threat to the Romulan Star Empire. His orders were clear. High Commander Tomalak himself had met with Seylok to brief him on this mission. Informants in Starfleet had confirmed that an artificial quantum singularity from an early Romulan prototype engine had been located. It was in orbit around a complex region of plasma storms the Federation referred to as the Badlands.

Seylok was ordered to proceed to the sector in the newly built scout ship to capture the AQS in an empty holding cell. The holding cell would be fitted in a specially adapted torpedo that he was to shoot into the wormhole. The scientists considered it an 84-percent probability that the passage of the volatile AQS through the wormhole would seal it shut.

At the end of their interview, Tomalak had admitted that Seylok had been raised to the rank of centurion and placed in charge of this mission to misdirect the shapeshifters. It was less likely infiltrating shapeshifters would focus on a low-priority mission headed by a newly made centurion.

Seylok braced his hand against one of the gray curved bulkheads. His ship, moving through space like a whispering bolt of energy—he could feel it, smell it in the air, surrounded by the aroma of success.

"Centurion!" Sublieutenant Retal announced. "Incoming message from Starfleet Outpost Gamma 12. They request our purpose. Shall I tell them—"

"I'll do it, sublieutenant," Seylok told her. He liked talking to top Starfleet brass. Besides, Tomalak had ordered him to be cooperative with Starfleet. They didn't want to raise any suspicions that this was a tactical mission. That's why only one small scout ship had been sent. The shapeshifters had proven they could infiltrate the ranks of Starfleet at will.

"This is Centurion Seylok," he said. "The *Bokra* is on course for the Badlands to test a new impulse-field variation."

The Starfleet commander shuffled some padds. "Oh, yes, I received word of your testing in the Badlands sector. Welcome to the Federation, Centurion."

"Thank you," Seylok told her. He so loved being called Centurion.

The screen returned to the starfield, slightly distorted by the warp field. "When will we arrive?" he asked.

"In approximately two days at top warp speed," Retal informed him.

"Very well." Seylok stood up. "I'll be in my quarters."

Seylok liked the way the crew watched him leave the bridge. He liked that he was the only one who knew their orders. There was even a confused impulse technician who right now was trying to figure out how their impulse engine was any different from ordinary impulse engines. Sublieutenant Jabak, the expert on AQS technology, hadn't yet seen the graviton generator and empty holding cell waiting in the cargo bay. No doubt he was wondering why he had been posted to a vessel that didn't have an AQS engine.

Seylok would tell select members of the crew their true mission only when they were nearing the Badlands. Tomalak had emphasized the need for strict secrecy, because the shapeshifters could be anywhere. If one of those creatures managed to get through the testing and the scans of the crew and ship, they would learn of his mission far too late to interfere.

Seylok had been waiting for a chance to shine, and he had learned patience. He was the only one who needed to know that he was about to change the fate of the Alpha Quadrant.

Chapter Three

THE CHANGELING went about its morning routine on DS9, just as it had done day after day for nearly a month, taking care of the solids and sometimes even saving their lives. The changeling was posing as Dr. Julian Bashir. The perfect cover: Dr. Bashir was the solid who performed the constant blood tests designed to detect changelings in the midst of the solids. The changeling had rigged the test to show real blood from both itself and the other undercover changeling on DS9.

The Bashir solid had been easy to duplicate, and the changeling had absorbed the medical knowledge it needed from the Great Link. Many centuries of posing as doctors among the solids had taught the Founders a great deal about solid anatomy. Once the wormhole had been discovered, they had infiltrated the various Alpha

Quadrant cultures and had amassed the medical knowledge they needed about humans, Bajorans, Klingons, Cardassians, Romulans, and various other humanoids. It was their nature to become familiar with everything they encountered, inside and out.

Odo entered sickbay, bidding him good morning.

The Bashir/changeling had to sternly control his instinctive reaction to reach out and merge with his fellow changeling. It hadn't been so difficult while Odo was still a solid. But since the baby changeling had infused its essence into Odo and he had become able to shape-change again, the pull to link had grown strong.

"What can I do for you, Odo?" the Bashir/changeling asked, in perfect imitation of the doctor's banter. "I thought I had seen the last of you after you regained your shape-shifting abilities."

Odo seemed embarrassed, remembering the petty aches and pains he had brought to the doctor while he was a solid. "It's about the baby changeling, doctor."

"Yes?" it asked, alerted.

"I have a proposal to make to Captain Sisko, but I'll need the medical records of the changeling."

The Bashir/changeling frowned slightly, remembering that the records on the baby changeling had been sent to Starfleet Headquarters. He sorely regretted giving any information about changelings to the solids; but in the end it would not matter. Soon the solids in the Alpha Quadrant would no longer be a problem. "What do you plan to do?" it asked.

"I want to find out what killed the changeling," Odo

said flatly. "I believe the Badlands anomaly caused the tetryon radiation poisoning."

The Bashir/changeling had never heard of the Badlands anomaly. "What if I come with you to talk to Captain Sisko?" it asked. "I can help explain what happened to the changeling."

"If . . . you're not too busy, doctor," Odo hedged. "This is a personal matter, after all."

"Not a problem," it replied, glad that the doctor was known to be a busybody. The changeling had to stay perfectly in character, or the Founders' invasion plan would be at risk.

As the Bashir/changeling followed Odo up to operations to talk to Captain Sisko, it once again regretted that minimal contact with field operatives meant that information made it back to the Founders slowly. The changeling hadn't been able yet to tell the others that Odo was a shape-shifter again. Eventually, the other changeling on DS9 would return to the Great Link and inform them.

The Jem'Hadar fleet was massing now in the Omarion Nebula on the other side of the wormhole, preparing to invade the Alpha Quadrant. It was only a matter of days until the invasion, at most a week. Until then, the changeling had to remain strictly undercover. It had its orders, and its part was too important to risk exposure now. It had been charged with keeping the wormhole open at any cost.

As Odo stepped onto ops, the Bashir/changeling covertly entered "Badlands anomaly" into its tricorder. It read most of the entry while Odo was requesting and receiving permission to speak to Captain Sisko.

In Sisko's office, the Bashir/changeling stood behind Odo while he explained to Captain Sisko that he wanted to use the *Defiant* to locate and trap the artificial quantum singularity that had been released long ago by the Romulan warbird.

"Since the baby changeling was found in the Badlands sector," Odo explained. "It was probably irradiated by tetryons from the AQS. Doctor?"

The Bashir/changeling stepped forward. "There's no doubt that the changeling died from tetryon radiation poisoning. I removed the isotopes and ran a level-one diagnostic. The tetryons had destabalized the morphogenic matrix of the baby changeling and irreparably damaged its cytoplasm."

Captain Sisko considered them. "So you know it encountered tetryon radiation—but how do you know the AQS caused the damage?"

"There are relatively few natural causes of tetryon radiation," the Bashir/changeling informed him.

"And I just found out that the baby changeling was found in the Badlands sector," Odo added, "near an area where the anomaly has been sighted."

Sisko shook his head, as if he wished Odo hadn't brought this to him. The Bashir/changeling wasn't surprised. Why should solids care if some anomaly was killing the Founders' young?

"How can we trap something that is in essence a microscopic black hole?" Sisko asked.

Odo placed a padd on his desk. "Lieutenant Commander Dax and Chief O'Brien say this device might work, sir."

"I see." Sisko picked up the padd, considering the technological wonder that had been created. "The *Defiant* just got back three hours ago."

"I spoke to Chief O'Brien last night, and he did most of the work with Dax via subspace communications."

"You must be very eager to take care of this problem, Constable."

"Sir, if any other changelings come through the Badlands, they also could suffer serious injury. Just like the last one did." Odo was too stiff to show emotion.

The Bashir/changeling pointed out, "Odo, since tetryon radiation is dangerous to changelings, it would be a risk for you to go into the area."

"It's a risk I have to take," Odo insisted. "We can't allow it to happen again."

The Bashir/changeling was warmed by Odo's concern for the young changeling that had been in his care. Odo's reaction went contrary to everything the Bashir/changeling knew about him through the Great Link. Odo was known to be reserved and introverted, shunning even his own people. Yet now the Bashir/changeling was witnessing Odo's slavish devotion to a tiny, defenseless changeling.

"So you want me to take the *Defiant* back to the Badlands?" Sisko asked. "To look for this AQS that nobody seems to be able to find?"

"Dax and O'Brien also worked on some sensor enhancements that might be able to detect tetryon radiation. I have the specs here." He handed Sisko another padd.

"You've really put some effort into this, Constable," Sisko said.

"Yes, sir." Odo hesitated, then added, "Captain Yates said last night that someone has to stop the AQS from hurting more life-forms. I agree."

"Kasidy said that?" Sisko asked. "Then I suppose she can't object if I miss her party this weekend."

"Then we can go?" Odo asked.

"Since this isn't an official mission, I'll have to ask for volunteers," Sisko reminded him. "If we get a full crew compliment, we can leave tomorrow morning."

The Bashir/changeling stepped forward. "Captain, request permission to join you. If you do encounter the Badlands anomaly, you'll need to have a doctor on board."

Sisko nodded. "Agreed."

The Bashir/changeling noted that Odo seemed very pleased. On the way out of ops, he even stopped by to talk to the Trill, Jadzia Dax, and the chief of operations, Miles O'Brien. Odo explained they would need volunteers in order to go on the mission.

The Bashir/changeling paused as Dax and Worf both volunteered. O'Brien and Kira wished them luck, but declined due to the recent birth of the human boy, Kirayoshi.

"Don't worry, Odo," Kira told him. "We'll make sure you have a crew."

Odo muttered and shuffled, unable to properly say thank you. But everyone seemed to understand.

The Bashir/changeling left when Odo elected to remain behind and work on the tetryon sensor matrix with Dax. The changeling's last glimpse was of Odo, Dax, and O'Brien hunched over the sensor diagnostic together.

On the way back down to sickbay, the changeling shook its head over the confusing situation. It was the changeling's considered opinion that the solids on board viewed Odo as a fellow solid, refusing to recognize his true nature.

Odo's behavior was more difficult to decipher. But it was not essential for the changeling to understand. It would link with its fellow changeling on board DS9 shortly after the Jem'Hadar fleet entered the Alpha Quadrant. Then the other changeling would rejoin the fleet and the Great Link, while the Bashir/changeling would complete its mission. Then everyone on this station would be gone, including itself, Odo, and all of the solids in the Bajoran sector.

In the Gamma Quadrant, on an ugly lump of an asteroid in an ugly part of space, Dominion internment camp number 371 was situated. The rocky prison had nothing to recommend it, with its vicious Jem'Hadar guards and its mixed bag of prisoners, from Romulans and Klingons to humans and the odd Ferengi or two.

Dr. Bashir had been captured by the Jem'Hadar on his way back from attending a burn-treatment conference on Meezan IV. He kept thinking about his friends on DS9. What had they thought when he hadn't returned? Were they still looking for him? Why had the Jem'Hadar made such an effort to capture him—

"They're coming!" hissed Varak. The Romulan woman moved from her post by the door.

Bashir quickly knocked twice on the panel leading to the crawlspace, to alert Enabran Tain. He had never imagined a situation in which he would be helping the leader of the Cardassian intelligence service. He wondered what Garak would have to say—if and when he ever got out of here. Bashir smiled, remembering how the Cardassian tailor had teased him with hints about the "secret Cardassian handshake" until Bashir had insisted Garak teach him how to do it. Garak still laughed about how gullible Bashir was back then.

The door hissed open, and several Jem'Hadar appeared, dragging General Martok. "He lost," one of them announced.

"How is he supposed to win when you beat him up day after day?" Bashir retorted.

General Martok hit the ground with a thud. Grunting, he tried to roll over as the Jem'Hadar turned and marched out of the cell.

Dr. Bashir hurried to his side. "Careful now," he urged. "Lie still while I examine you." He didn't have a medical tricorder, but he could tell that Martok's arm was broken by the way his body flinched when he tried to adjust it.

"Your arm is broken, General. You can't fight anymore—"

"Honor demands that I fight!" Martok wheezed.

Bashir pressed him down. "Not tomorrow, anyway. Or the next day. Do you want a compound fracture?" Bashir examined his arm more thoroughly, letting that prove his point.

Martok's eyes rolled back. Even Klingons had a level beyond which they could not tolerate pain. Martok had been physically abused for nearly two years. Bashir hated to think what a medical scan would reveal.

"Help me get him onto the bed," Bashir told Janok, the other Romulan in their cell. Together they carried the half-unconscious Klingon to his cot. Martok protested the entire time, but the old warrior was nearing the end of his strength.

The knocking inside the wall alerted Janok, who opened the small panel with the prybar. He had to stretch his arm down to knock the larger panel out. It took several hard blows for Janok to get it open.

The Romulan complained over his shoulder to Bashir, "I don't know how you do it so easily."

"There's a trick to everything," Bashir said with a shrug. He had quietly taken over opening the difficult panel, while continuing to conceal his superior strength, gained through forbidden genetic enhancements. He was glad to have the advantage in this place.

Enabran Tain emerged from the hole, shaking his head. Bashir had investigated the crawlspace one time while Tain was being interrogated. You had to crawl through the hole and sort of slide up between the walls. It was maddeningly narrow.

"It's about time," Bashir told him. "You should rest once in a while."

"Rest!" General Martok exclaimed in disgust from his prone position. "Work *harder*, Cardassian!"

As usual, Tain ignored the Klingon. He went over to

the spigot and turned on the water. He doused his head with it.

Bashir knew the lack of humidity was bothering the old Cardassian spymaster. And the chill air. What a way to end your life, stuck in a narrow crawlspace trying to rewire an old environmental control system into a transmitter. Martok said that Tain had been trying to modify the former life-support system for over a year, wiring the message and transmission coordinates directly into the system's circuitry. Once it was completed, Tain planned to connect the transmitter to the power grid and let it run.

Tain shook the water from his head. With the panel closed, Varak moved away from the door.

"When will it be completed?" Varak asked.

"Perhaps never," Tain retorted. His heavy-set face was streaming with water. "Perhaps in a few days."

Bashir sighed. Tain had said that last time he asked about his progress. Even though they all cooperated, and everyone would die if the crawl space was discovered, Tain didn't trust any of them.

Bashir went over to Tain. "May I?" he asked, before taking the Cardassian's pulse in his neck ridge. It was uneven and faint, as it had been since the doctor had arrived. Enabran Tain's heart was failing.

"You must rest," Bashir quietly told him. "If you don't, you'll die."

"I am dying, doctor." Tain wheezed and could hardly draw a full breath. "That is the problem with you *humans,* you value life far too much."

"I'm a doctor," Bashir replied. "It's my job to save people's lives."

"Not mine," Tain retorted.

"Nor mine!" Martok suddenly agreed from across the room.

There was a silence in the cell. Then the two old men began to chuckle through their pain.

"I'm glad you've both found something to amuse you," Bashir said sourly. But he was pleased that they were agreeing on something. He was beginning to see that there was a deep respect between them, though they were barely civil to one another.

Bashir returned to his cot. As long as both of them were relaxing, he could relax. He wasn't sure how much longer either of them could hold out. The two Romulans in the cell were more likely to die of boredom, and who knows what the Breen felt? The Breen just sat there day after day, never uttering a sound.

Bashir still couldn't understand why he had been abducted. The Jem'Hadar had simply told him, "You are an enemy of the Dominion." Perhaps he was in the wrong place at the wrong time. But Bashir couldn't accept that. Meezan IV wasn't near any strategic target, and the Jem'Hadar were too focused for anything to be an accident.

Besides, their interrogation had been too thorough. They knew everything about his routines on board DS9, right down to the way he threw darts. But the interrogations had stopped a week ago; Bashir was relieved. The drugs the Vorta used to loosen his tongue had been extremely unpleasant. He had babbled about the minutiae of his life whether they asked for it or not, determined to hide his knowledge of the forbidden transmitter Tain was working on.

One thing he was sure of—Captain Sisko would never think to search for him in the Gamma Quadrant, deep in Dominion territory. If Tain's transmitter didn't work, he could be here for a very long time.

Chapter Four

DAX WAS GLAD that so many crewmembers had volunteered to join the *Defiant* in their search for the artificial quantum singularity. Some of the scientists were eager to participate in the research mission; an even greater number were going just because they wanted to help Odo.

Of course, Odo didn't know how to deal with it. He seemed embarrassed when his friends wished him well before they left DS9.

Even now, Odo was standing some distance behind Sisko's chair, not wanting to intrude on their jobs. But his interest showed, as he tried to see what everyone was doing.

"Entering the Badlands sector," Dax announced from the helm.

"Is your tetryon sensor net prepared?" Sisko asked.

"Ready to go, Captain," Dax agreed, adjusting course.

She and O'Brien had created a sensor net the *Defiant* could use to "drag" the area around the Badlands. It was a sphere of space that spread for nearly 2 million kilometers around the *Defiant*.

No one had ever tried this method before. It was a classic case of bureaucratic secrecy interfering with science, since it was nearly two years since Captain Janeway had theorized that an artificial quantum singularity was in orbit around the Badlands. Several months after that the crew of DS9 had discovered a way to track the tetryon emissions from the engine of a Romulan warbird even when it was cloaked.

However, since the DS9 method dealt with piercing the Romulan cloaking technology, it had been classified on a need-to-know basis. None of the science vessels that had subsequently searched for the AQS in the Badlands had heard of the new sensor technique.

Then the Klingons had attacked Cardassia, and the Maquis had taken over the Badlands sector. No Starfleet science ships had ventured into the region since.

Dax was excited about their mission. She liked to try new things, and it was even better when she could help out a friend at the same time.

"Search pattern entered," Worf announced.

"Proceed," Sisko ordered.

"First coordinates received," Dax confirmed. She smiled at Worf but—typically—he was in "officer mode" and didn't return her grin. She didn't care. Having him along was all she wanted.

Worf had immediately volunteered, even before she did. He seemed to relish the opportunity to return to the Badlands, where Maquis were still to be found. Besides, Worf preferred being on the *Defiant,* and he took any excuse for ship duty.

"Initiating the sensor net," Dax announced.

"The power grid is stable," Worf reported. "I am increasing the bandwidth."

Dax watched the sensor feed expand as extra bandwidth was added. Though O'Brien had helped create the sensor net and the trap, he hadn't come along on this mission. She wasn't surprised. Kira had offered to return to the spare room in O'Brien's quarters to help care for the infant Kirayoshi, but everyone could see how difficult it was for Kira to separate herself from the baby. So O'Brien had stayed.

Dax had overheard O'Brien apologize to Odo, "I wish I could help. If something hurt my kids, I'd sure want to find it and stop it."

Odo had harrumphed and muttered, "Yes, of course, Chief. You have other responsibilities." But Dax thought it meant more to Odo than he admitted.

"Sensor net fully extended," Dax reported. "Reading slightly higher levels of tetryon particles than usual. Distribution appears random."

"Probably old emissions from the AQS," Odo commented.

Dr. Bashir was seated at the science station. "The

level of tetryons is not high enough to produce tetryon radiation."

"Well, that's reassuring," Captain Sisko drawled.

"Let's hope it stays that way," Bashir murmured.

"A spike in the levels would indicate the AQS is nearby," Dax reminded everyone. They didn't need to be so cautious they forgot their objective.

"When we do find it," Sisko continued, "we won't have much time. Is the subspace trap ready?"

"Aye, Captain," Worf replied. "But I wish we had the opportunity to test it."

"We know that the subspace interphase pocket forms when we trigger the field inverter," Dax protested. "We just won't know if it will act as a trap until we put the AQS inside it."

"Exactly," Worf retorted.

Dax smiled. "You find me a microscopic black hole, and we'll test the interphase pocket, Worf. But the only tiny black hole I know about is the AQS somewhere here in the Badlands."

Sisko calmly interjected, "You two don't exactly inspire me with confidence."

"It'll work, Captain," Dax assured him, giving Worf a cautioning look. They had discussed the problems before leaving DS9, but this was their best shot.

"We will make it work," Worf flatly agreed.

Odo was moving in closer to Bashir at the science station. The doctor pointed out, "This is the graph that follows tetryon emissions. Since tetryons are subspace particles moving at the equivalent of our warp 9.99, there is only a slight delay—which is shown here."

Odo nodded stiffly, starting to withdraw politely.

"Any time," the doctor offered. "I know you're concerned."

Odo hesitated, then said, "Thank you." He looked around the bridge. "All of you. Thank you for helping me do this."

"Always glad to be of help," Captain Sisko replied, smiling. He looked relaxed, better than Dax had seen him in months.

There was a chorus of "Ah, it's nothing" from the crew, and Dax thought it was downright cute the way Odo reacted. Poor thing, he really had a hard time getting close to people.

"This AQS has to be stopped," Dr. Bashir assured Odo. "And it's about time we did it. We shouldn't have waited so long."

Odo nodded, appeased by the notion that it was their duty to stop the AQS.

"One full rotation of the search pattern has been completed," Worf announced, all business as usual. "Commencing repetition of the pattern."

Dax smiled to herself. Why was she so fond of all these uptight men? Maybe because she knew they felt the same way she did, only they didn't think it was right to show it. If they weren't adventurers, they wouldn't be working on the edge of known space at the doorway to an unknown quadrant.

So Dax didn't mind when Worf was sometimes too serious about his work. It was just the way he dealt with life—like Torias, her fifth host. That poor young man didn't know how to be anything but intense. With his work as well as his relationships. Nilani Kahn . . . ah, the grand passion. That was what Worf wanted, while Dax . . . she just wanted Worf.

She winked at him when he glanced up. His expression softened. *That's my Klingon,* she thought, returning to her work. Life was very good right now, and after seven lifetimes of experience, Dax knew enough to enjoy every second of it while it lasted.

"Five hundred and twenty-five full rotations of the search pattern have been completed," Commander Worf announced. "Commencing repetition of the pattern."

Captain Sisko put his hand to his forehead. Many hours ago, he had requested that Worf cease announcing each completed rotation. The commander was now only announcing every twenty-five completed rotations. His inflection never varied. Sisko got the feeling that Worf would continue to perform the search pattern for the next several weeks—while everyone else slowly died of boredom.

Dax paused next to the captain's command chair, her raktajino cup in hand. "You want another one, Benjamin?"

Sisko slowly looked over at her. "It's not working, is it, Old Man?"

Dax hesitated, then shrugged. "It could take days to find it, Benjamin. Even though we've isolated our search to a corridor where we estimate the AQS is in orbit, we can't spread the net at warp speed."

"Days . . ." Sisko watched as Odo leaned over Bashir's shoulder, monitoring the sensor activity.

"Even weeks." Dax smiled and shrugged as if he should have known what to expect. Sisko had to admit the commander's assessment had been honest, if a trifle enthusiastic. Dax headed to the back of the bridge to get a refill.

"Sir!" Worf called out. "There is a vessel on long-range sensors."

"On screen," Sisko ordered. His arm console displayed the incoming trajectory. It wasn't a normal approach from either the Federation or from Cardassian space. Perhaps a stray Maquis?

"It is a Romulan scout ship," Worf informed him. "Approaching at warp 7."

"Yellow alert," Sisko ordered, prepared to take no chances.

"Shields up," Worf announced.

The flashing alert signal caught everyone by surprise, but even Dax was back at her station before Sisko could give the order. "Disengage search pattern. Helm, take us into the sensor shadow, but stay within our search corridor."

"Aye, sir," Dax replied, inputting his commands.

The Badlands grew on the viewscreen until the interference began to appear as static. Sisko followed the trajectory of the Romulan ship. It appeared they hadn't seen the *Defiant,* as it sank deeper into the sensor shadow.

"Direct our enhanced sensors at the Romulan vessel," Sisko ordered. They would need everything to punch through the sensor shadow.

After a few minutes, Worf announced, "Romulan

scout ship closing. Weapons are still off-line. It is approximately the same mass as the *Defiant,* with similar armament capacity."

"A small, fast, strong ship," Sisko mused. When he looked at their first sensor image of the ship, it seemed different from the usual Romulan scout vessel. Obviously the Romulans had picked up a thing or two from installing the cloaking device on the *Defiant* a year ago. The admirals at Starfleet Headquarters were going to be interested in this development.

"They better drop out of warp soon," Dax commented. "Or we're all going to get some unpleasant reverberation waves when they hit the sensor shadow."

"Boosting power to the shields," Worf confirmed.

After a tense moment or two, Dr. Bashir said, "Seems their captain heard you. They're dropping out of warp."

Sisko narrowed his eyes at how close they had cut it. The Romulan commander either liked to make a flashy entrance or he was inexperienced.

"The scout ship is changing course!" Worf warned. "Entering the sensor shadow. It is on an intercept course and closing on our location at full impulse power."

So the *Defiant* had been seen.

The last dealings Sisko had with Romulans was right after a bomb blast that killed twenty-seven people at the conference between the Romulan and Federation governments on Earth. The Dominion had planned their sabotage well. Despite all their efforts to continue discussions leading toward an alliance against the Dominion, the Romulans had withdrawn in silence to their vast territory. Relations had been frosty ever since.

Sisko clenched his teeth over the cost of that one slip in security. The Romulans believed that the Federation was doomed if Dominion agents could infiltrate the very heart of Starfleet. And Sisko could hardly blame them.

"Hail them," Sisko ordered impatiently. He didn't have time to play games. The *Defiant* had a cloaking device given to Starfleet through a special treaty with the Romulans. Last time Sisko checked, they were still allies.

"Channel open," Worf confirmed.

Sisko sat forward as an image of the bridge of the Romulan scout appeared. "Captain Sisko of the Federation Starship *Defiant*."

"Centurion Seylok of the *Bokra*."

The Romulan was quite young, yet he had an arrogant lift to his chin.

"Nice ship, Centurion," Sisko commented. "Looks new."

"The *Bokra* was just commissioned," Seylok said with a sardonic smile.

Sisko could have sworn Seylok understood his allusion to its similarity to the *Defiant*. "You're a long way from home, Centurion."

"We are here to test a variation on the subspace field grid in our impulse engines," Belok explained. "It should enable our ship to pass unscathed through the plasma storms. But of course you know that."

"No . . . ," Sisko said. "How could I know that?"

"The Romulan Star Empire received permission

from Starfleet Headquarters to allow our passage through Federation space to the Badlands sector." Seylok looked smug. "I assume you are here to watch us."

"You assume wrong," Sisko said shortly. He tapped out a quick message to Worf to confirm what Centurion Seylok was saying. Out of the corner of his eye, he saw Worf nod acknowledgment. "I know nothing about Romulans field-testing impulse engines in the Badlands,"

"Oh?" Seylok asked, clearly not believing him. "Then why are you here?"

Sisko glanced around the bridge. "We're on a scientific research mission."

Seylok grinned outright at that. He didn't bother to hide his disbelief. "And Starfleet just happened to send the *Defiant* on a *science* mission when a Romulan ship was scheduled to be in the sector. . . ."

Sisko was cursing his defensive position when Worf transmitted confirmation of Seylok's claim. Starfleet Headquarters had approved field testing by the *Bokra*. Sisko hadn't been notified because Starfleet Headquarters had only just gotten word of his decision to return to the Badlands sector to conduct a search for the AQS. So much for unofficial missions.

"Ah, Captain," Seylok assured him. "The Romulan Star Empire expected something like this. Your overtures of friendship extend only so far before distrust takes over."

"It's a large sector," Sisko told him dryly. "I'm sure we won't get in each other's way."

Seylok started to say, "Let's hope not—"

"Captain Sisko!" Bashir exclaimed. "Tetryon levels—"

The *Defiant* was jolted by a shock wave. Captain Sisko felt himself lift from the command chair. He hung on, but instead of resettling, he lifted higher. The lights dimmed.

"Artificial gravity off-line!" Dr. Bashir called out.

Sisko couldn't see much, while he was busy trying to hang onto the back of the chair. But he tried to count out the seconds. He reached "five" when the gravity recommenced and he fell to the deck. Immediately he rolled to look at the viewscreen. It showed a gray interference pattern.

"Report," the captain ordered. His breath came short, and there was a sharp pain in his side where he had hit the back of the chair. He leaned over the tender spot as he awkwardly stood up, reaching for his seat. Probably a broken rib or two.

"Sir, auxiliary power is holding," Worf reported. "We should have main power in a few minutes."

"There's some circuitry damage with impulse power, but that should be fixed in a few minutes," Dax added, checking the helm control. "Warp drive was off-line and is undamaged."

"Sensors are off-line," Dr. Bashir reported. "Including the sensor net. It was focused on the Romulan vessel, so we didn't have much warning."

Sisko sat down in the command chair. "Agh!" he couldn't help exclaiming.

"Sir, are you all right?" Bashir asked.

Impatiently, Sisko waved away the doctor's concern. "What was our level of radiation exposure?"

"Moderate," Bashir reported. "I'm monitoring the levels of free radicals forming in the *Defiant's* atmosphere. It will take time to see if the chief's redaction shielding screened out the tetryon radiation."

"Have the triage teams administer cellular regeneration treatments," Sisko ordered. They had come prepared for this. "Worf, what about the Romulans?"

"The *Bokra* is within visual range," Worf replied. "On screen."

The viewscreen returned to the starfield. In the distance, the scout ship caught the light from the nearby plasma storms.

"Magnify," Sisko ordered.

The image sprang closer. Now the scout ship's flared bow was tilted up relative to the *Defiant*.

"Thrusters are engaged," Worf reported. "They are holding the ship in place against the gravity pull of the Badlands."

"Benjamin, they just came out of warp," Dax reminded him. "Their subspace generator was probably still on-line. The shockwave must have overloaded their power conduits."

"Hail them," Sisko ordered. The *Defiant* had taken their warp core off-line when they entered the Badlands sector, just one of several precautions they had taken in case they encountered the AQS. Sisko could tell by the indicator lights that full impulse power would be restored momentarily.

"Channel open," Worf confirmed. "Audio only."

Sisko had to imagine what the bridge of the *Bokra* looked like. He could hear the hissing of ruptured conduits through the open channel. "Centurion Seylok, do you require assistance?"

Muffled shouting that sounded like barked orders returned.

"Centurion Seylok?" Sisko asked again.

"Sensors back on-line, Captain," Bashir reported. "The *Bokra* is on emergency life-support."

"All main power systems have been compromised," Worf agreed from the tactical station. "No ion wake, no power spikes."

"Is there any danger of a warp-core breach?" Sisko asked.

"Negative," Worf responded. "Warp systems have been shut down."

"Move in," Sisko told Dax.

"Approaching at one-quarter impulse power," she acknowledged.

Sisko sat back, listening to the sounds of an emergency situation on board the *Bokra,* until the channel was abruptly closed. He shifted gingerly, not wanting to jolt his sore ribs. He wasn't too worried about Seylok and his crew—they knew where to find the *Defiant* if they needed help.

"Why all the long faces, people?" In spite of the pain, Sisko grinned around the bridge. "I'd say we've found what we were looking for."

Chapter Five

THE BASHIR/CHANGELING left his post on the bridge to tend to the solids on board the *Defiant*. First, it repaired Captain Sisko's cracked ribs and a host of minor injuries suffered by the bridge crew during the gravity loss. The changeling also treated the solids for the tetryon irradiation they had received.

Tetryon neutrinos, like all neutrinos, were the most penetrating of subatomic particles, because they reacted with matter only through the force of weak interaction, like radioactive decay. The ship's systems suffered far less permanent damage than the solids did. Several of the humanoids received doses of nearly 400 rads, despite their precautions, such as employing a variable overlap redaction in the shield cycles.

Still, the Bashir/changeling was impressed. Despite their proximity to the AQS when it passed, only

10 percent of the crew was seriously injured, compared to a 50 percent serious injury rate on the Cardassian ship *Vetar*.

The changeling called Odo into sickbay as soon as it could. It needed to find out if its own cytoplasm had been damaged by the tetryon particles. The only way to do that was to run a scan of its morphogenic matrix while scanning Odo.

Odo was not pleased to be pulled away from the bridge. "Can't this wait, Doctor? We're attempting to run a locator simulation to determine where and when the AQS will pass by the same coordinates again."

"I can tell you right now," the Bashir/changeling said, ushering Odo toward his work table.

"You can?" Odo asked in surprise.

"Yes, it will take days for it to orbit the Badlands even at warp 9.99. That gives you plenty of time to hop in that jar and let me take some readings on you." The Bashir/changeling gestured toward the large beaker seated on the computer diagnostic sensor.

Odo glanced at the doctor, reluctant—as well he might be—to revert to a gelatinous state in front of a solid.

"Come on, Odo," it urged exactly as Bashir would do, teasing and patronizing at the same time. "It's the not the first time. I'll have you out of there in no time."

Odo looked distinctly uncomfortable. "Oh, all right."

He pointed his hands at the glass beaker and poured himself into it. The Bashir/changeling didn't let its charade falter, not by a gesture or change in expression. Odo was, perhaps, not the most proficient changeling in the galaxy, but he could perceive his surroundings quite well while he was in the gelatinous state.

The Bashir/changeling took a sample of Odo. When it turned its back on the large beaker, it poured some of itself into a test tube on the counter. Now it had two samples to run. It carefully set the two test tubes of cytoplasm apart from each other. The changeling couldn't afford to make a mistake and try to absorb Odo's sample. That would alert Odo.

The Bashir/changeling wouldn't have taken the risk, but if it had been irreparably damaged by the tetryon radiation, the Founders would have to be notified immediately. His part in the planned invasion was too important.

The diagnostic medical scan was still underway when the comm whistled. *"Sisko to Dr. Bashir."*

"Bashir, here."

"Doctor, how's Odo?"

"I'm running the scan now, Captain." Bashir managed to sound properly grave, yet hopeful of a good outcome.

"Keep me informed. Sisko out."

Odo would undoubtedly be grateful for the captain's display of concern. The changeling understood that solids could sometimes be astonishingly kind and altruistic. Like now, the way they were helping Odo track down the AQS because it hurt his baby changeling.

But solids inevitably turned against those they loved the most, often for obscure, idiosyncratic reasons. The solids were good to Odo now, but it would take very little, the changeling was sure, for their trust to be withdrawn.

The medical scan signaled when it was completed. The Bashir/changeling switched the test tubes and placed its own sample in the scanner. The scan was set to run twice for redundancy.

While its own sample was being diagnosed, the changeling examined the results of Odo's scan. There were biomimetic fluctuations in Odo's morphogenic matrix.

The changeling glanced over at the large beaker of Odo. The fluctuations were moderate compared to those of the baby changeling. But time and the free radicals still loose inside the *Defiant* would cause them to escalate.

When the second scan was completed, the Bashir/changeling was glad to see that its own morphogenic matrix was stable. The Bashir/changeling had been sitting right next to Odo on the bridge, and the difference was substantial. Thereby proving the purely random nature of tetryon radiation.

The Bashir/changeling reabsorbed its own sample before returning Odo's portion to him. After pouring it back in, the changeling ran an insomatic inductor over the entire mass. It took several minutes for the treatment cycle to complete.

"You can come out now, Odo." The changeling cross-checked the scans with the inductor readings as Odo reformed. The changeling remembered to shift uneasily, as all solids instinctively did whenever a Founder reformed nearby. That natural response to draw away had colored their response to nonsolids since the beginning of time, when the changelings had founded their ancient civilization.

"You've been exposed to tetryon radiation," the Bashir/changeling told Odo. "The damage doesn't appear to be serious. You're not nearly at the levels the baby changeling was exposed to. I can treat you with insomatic inductions to stabilize your biomimetic fluctuations. I've already given you your first treatment. Report back here in two hours for your second. We'll know in a day or two if there will be any long-term effects."

"As long as it's not serious," Odo said impatiently. "The captain wanted me to return to the bridge, Doctor. May I go now?"

"Odo, this could be serious. If you get exposed again—and since we're chasing after that thing, you're bound to be exposed again—it will raise the level of isotopes in your cytoplasm." The Bashir/changeling had no difficulty sounding sincere. "I suggest you and I return to DS9 with the three most seriously wounded crew members. The others can finish the job now."

"No thank you, Doctor." Odo continued out the door. "I'll arrange for the shuttlecraft to be prepared if you need to return with the others. But I'm staying right here."

"You could be making a big mistake," the Bashir/changeling called after him.

But Odo merely waved one hand, uninterested in his own personal danger. The changeling could almost admire his single-minded quest to stop the thing that had killed the baby changeling. But it knew that Odo also refused just because he had to be contrary. He was one of those rare changelings who didn't want to join with the others. Odo wanted to be an individual, a singular entity, and even now that he was a changeling again he was off chasing after anomalies—rather than running as fast as he could back to his own people to join in the Great Link.

The Bashir/changeling shook its head glumly. Now it couldn't return to DS9. There was no one else qualified to monitor Odo's morphogenic matrix and make sure he got his induction treatments. No matter how much Odo had shunned the Founders, they still loved him as much as he had loved that sick baby changeling.

Commander Worf kept a close watch on the sensor readings of the *Bokra*. He was disturbed by the silence from the Romulan scout ship. It seemed unlikely that the ship was so badly damaged their communications array was still down.

Finally they received the signal Worf had been expecting. "Captain, we are being hailed by the *Bokra*."

"Put it on screen," Sisko ordered.

Centurion Seylok stood with his back to the screen. Steam still billowed from several conduits, obscuring the other figures working over their command consoles.

Seylok slowly turned, holding his arms out from his sides, palms up. His stiff woven uniform was charred black across one shoulder down to his chest.

"Are you satisfied, Captain Sisko?" Seylok asked darkly.

"This damage was none of our doing, Centurion," Sisko quickly protested.

Seylok slammed his hand down on the nearest console. "An unprovoked attack! Romulus will hear about this!"

Worf felt his blood grow hotter in response. The Romulan intended to fight!

Sisko didn't lose his cool. "We did not attack you, Centurion Seylok. The shockwave came from something we call the Badlands anomaly. The systems on the *Defiant* were also affected."

Seylok crossed his arms. "You have impulse power! You have sensors and shields. We are nearly adrift. Explain that."

"We took precautions because we know the Badlands anomaly has been sighted in this area." Sisko quickly added, "We can give you the proper shield harmonics to help protect your crew from the tetryon radiation, should you encounter it again."

Seylok was still angry. "Whatever the cause, you have us at your mercy. What are your terms?"

"Terms?" Sisko repeated. "You mean surrender? We didn't attack you, Centurion. But we'd be willing to help you get your ship back in working order."

Seylok hesitated. Several of the figures in the mist moved closer, listening. "You are willing to assist us with repairs?"

"Tell us what you need," Sisko assured him.

Worf felt disappointed. Somehow, it did not seem right. The volatile situation had been defused too easily. Worf seriously considered the possibility that the Romulan was trying to deceive them.

But Captain Sisko continued to work out the details of sending over a repair crew to assess damage. Worf was very interested in seeing the interior of an advanced Romulan scout ship. And his suspicions were too vague for him to protest Sisko's plans. But he was determined to remain vigilant.

Worf noted when Odo returned, as he took note of everyone who entered and left the bridge. Though Odo paused in the rear, Centurion Seylok also saw him. In the middle of Captain Sisko's sign off the Centurion raised an accusing finger. "A shape-shifter!"

Seylok's voice was filled with loathing, and Worf felt a chill. This was not fakery. Seylok wanted to punch through the screen to reach Odo. Yet Worf also believed that Seylok's rage was all the higher because he knew he was safe on the other side of a comm link.

"Murdering *vorson!*" Seylok bellowed.

"Centurion Seylok!" Sisko rebuked. "Odo is my chief of security on DS9. You will treat him with the respect due my entire crew."

Seylok seemed surprised at his own outburst. Worf saw the centurion's uncertainty. "As you wish, Captain," Seylok finally muttered, giving Odo one last scathing look.

Sisko settled back in his command chair as the screen returned to the starfield. Commander Worf made notations in the console for his relief, and turned, ready for orders. The tension on the bridge was high from Seylok's outburst.

"Commander Worf, take Dax and Rom with you to see what repairs are most pressing on the *Bokra.*"

"Aye, sir," Worf agreed, but he couldn't help wishing the captain had not named the Ferengi.

Odo crossed his arms, leaning against a bulkhead. "I don't suppose I'm on the away team?"

"I think not," Sisko agreed. "You can take the tactical station. Keep a lock on the away team at all times. And try to stay out of Seylok's sight, from now on. Perhaps he had friends in the Tal Shiar . . ."

". . . who died when the Dominion ambushed their joint mission with the Cardassians," Odo finished. "Undoubtedly."

Rom hurried up to the bridge from engineering and arrived panting. "Did somebody call me?"

Dax handed him an engineering kit. "We're going."

"Where to?" Rom asked, confused.

"The Romulan scout ship," Dax gleefully told him, picking up an engineering kit of her own. She looked excited about the idea.

"Romulan ship . . ." Rom's eyes grew wider and he deliberately swallowed. But he put the strap of the kit over his shoulder without another word.

Sisko addressed the three members of the away team. "Say as little as possible about the Badlands anomaly. We don't want any interference from the Romulans."

"The AQS won't complete its orbit for nearly three days," Dax offered. "We've got plenty of time for the calibration program to complete. Then we can set up the trap on precisely the right coordinates and retreat to a safe distance."

"Good," Sisko said. "Then our top priority now is to repair that Romulan scout ship so it can leave the area."

"Understood, sir," Worf acknowledged.

Worf led the away team to the transporter pads behind the bridge. He wasn't pleased with his away team. The Ferengi's mouth was hanging open stupidly, and Jadzia was almost laughing on the way back to the transporter pads.

"You must be on your guard," Worf quietly told her. "I do not trust this Romulan."

"Oh?" Dax asked. "I thought he seemed quite charming. Maybe it was those pointed ears. They get me every time."

Worf glared at her. "You must take this seriously, Jadzia. It could be dangerous."

"Dangerous!" Rom exclaimed. The Ferengi stopped in his tracks, blocking the way. "Nobody said anything about it being dangerous."

Irritated, Worf realized Rom had overheard him even though he had only meant to speak to Dax. He must learn not to underestimate those huge Ferengi ears.

"You're scaring Rom," Dax told him. "Besides, I bet I've been on more Romulan ships than you have."

Since Worf had never boarded a Romulan vessel, he ignored her comment. They stepped onto the transporter pad.

"Away team ready?" he asked.

Rom acknowledged, "I guess so," while Jadzia said, "Let her rip."

Containing his impatience, Worf nodded to the transporter chief. "Ready for transport."

The familiar walls of the *Defiant* dissolved as the transporter beamed them to the *Bokra*.

Dax took a deep breath. "Romulan!" she murmured, moving closer behind Worf.

Worf had fought with Jadzia a few weeks ago, when she had claimed that she could tell which life-forms crewed a vessel simply from the smell. Worf had argued that it was impossible due to modern air-purification methods. But he had to agree there was a pungent tang to this air that he had never encountered before.

"Greetings," said the Romulan crewmember at the transporter controls. "Centurion Seylok will be here shortly."

Worf stepped off the transporter pads. The Romulan ship was disorienting. The walls were not solid, but were made of metal screens, some with tiny holes and others with fist-sized openings. He could see into the corridor between the transporter room and engineering. The computer core was on one side, and the back half of the ship was a vast hall several levels high containing the warp core. The low light and layered screens kept him from seeing clearly, but movement showed that repairs were underway. The sound of strained systems was unmistakable.

From the other direction, several Romulans were approaching. He recognized the form of Centurion Seylok even through the screens. He was a slender humanoid, smaller in stature than the Romulan honor guard preceding him. Their uniforms were streamlined and less bulky than the military uniforms worn by the crew of a Romulan warship, but made of the same metallic mesh.

As they entered the transporter nook, Centurion Seylok said, "Excuse the delay. We are hardly in any shape to receive visitors."

"This is the repair team," Worf corrected. "I am Commander Worf, this is Commander Dax, and this is Junior Grade Technician Rom."

"Welcome on board the *Bokra*." Seylok was looking from one to the other. "A Klingon, a Ferengi, and a Trill. How . . . Starfleet."

Worf's spine stiffened in resentment, though it was only the Romulan's tone that implied insult.

But Dax was smiling. "That's one of the best things about Starfleet, Centurion. Getting to work with people from different cultures and backgrounds."

"I'm sure that's true." Seylok stepped closer to her. "I must admit I've always been curious about Trill. They say that you live forever."

Dax laughed. "Not quite. But some joined Trill have the memories of many lifetimes."

"Do you?" Seylok asked.

"My symbiont has had seven hosts."

Seylok's gaze became more intrigued. "Fascinating. . . ."

Worf didn't like it. "We are here to begin repairs on the *Bokra*."

"Indeed," Seylok agreed, still smiling at Dax. "You are a technician?"

"Just show me what needs fixing," Dax told him, patting the repair kit.

Seylok gestured to the door. "This way."

Much to Worf's irritation, Seylok kept Dax next to him as they walked into the corridor. He had to follow behind with the Ferengi. Dax shot him an apologetic glance, but Worf could tell she was enjoying herself. She wasn't encouraging Seylok's attention, but she apparently appreciated it.

Grimly, Worf kept his mind on duty. He noted that the interior layout of the *Bokra* was much like that of the *Defiant*. The engine design was similar, based on antimatter technology rather than incorporating an AQS, like the enormous Romulan warbirds. The weapons banks were concealed behind bulkheads.

Worf tried to look everywhere but in front of him, as Seylok and Dax had a spirited conversation. Rom peered around as much as Worf, but he acted like a frightened, stupid sheep.

"Close your mouth," Worf ordered under his breath.

"Huh?" Rom asked. "Oh . . . sor-ry."

Seylok lead them into the engineering section, toward a group of Romulan technicians. Their metallic-mesh jumpsuits were charred in places, as were the screens separating the work stations from the plasma-injector system. Panels were open everywhere with charred ODN wire hanging down.

One side of the power transfer conduit was open, revealing the taps for the electroplasma system. All that was left of the taps were blackened masses.

Dax took one look and asked, "Do you have any taps that are intact?"

"None," the lead technician replied.

"You do have the specs on file?" Dax asked hopefully.

"Yes," Seylok assured her. "We can get you a copy." He flicked one finger at a technician, who hurried over to a computer terminal.

"What is the source of your emergency power?" Worf asked.

Seylok answered, "Auxiliary fusion generators."

The technician quickly returned with a narrow computer chip. He handed it to his commander with a salute. Worf noted the military precision of their interaction, even on a nonmilitary science vessel.

Worf reached out, but Seylok handed the chip to Dax. "We don't have much auxiliary fuel left."

Dax turned to Worf and handed him the chip. "We're going to have to replicate new EPS taps on board the *Defiant*. I'll stay here and start dismantling the conduit system. Send over the taps as they're produced."

Worf didn't like the position she had placed him in. "Rom can go."

Rom reached out for the computer chip, but Dax shook her head. "I need Rom to help me here. Now, be sure half of those taps are high-energy and the other half are low-power input."

Worf glanced down at the chip in his hand. Seylok was smiling at Dax again in a particularly intimate and offensive way. "Would you like to see the other power conduit?"

"Yes, Centurion," Dax said, gesturing for Rom to follow.

Worf knew that he didn't want to leave Jadzia with-

Susan Wright

out security simply because she was his Par'machkai. Yet he couldn't allow his feelings to interfere with his duty. So he touched his comm badge, and said, "Commander Worf to *Defiant.* One to return."

His last view of the Romulan vessel was of Seylok's hand rising to Jadzia's back, assisting her over some fallen debris. Worf growled low in his throat as he dematerialized.

Chapter Six

MAJOR KIRA thought it was an interesting turn of events when Captain Sisko contacted DS9 to report that they were assisting the Romulans. She always knew the Romulans would reemerge some day. The Dominion had beaten them back from the Gamma Quadrant, but they hadn't beaten them.

On the console viewscreen in ops, Captain Sisko finished his summary with, *"We hope to have the Bokra repaired in another day or so."*

Kira was shaking her head in doubt. "Why would the Romulans go all the way to the Badlands just to test an impulse engine? That doesn't sound right."

"I agree," he said simply.

"Do you think they know about the AQS?" Kira asked.

"I think anything is possible," Sisko told her. *"Com-*

mander Worf says the Bokra is nearly identical to the Defiant."

"Well, what do you know . . . ," O'Brien said from his ops station. He sounded pleased with the idea that the Romulans had copied their successful design.

"I'll keep you informed of our progress," Sisko told her.

"Good luck," Kira told him as she signed off.

"A Romulan ship!" O'Brien muttered. "I wish I was there. Last time I was on a Romulan ship, I was posted to the *Enterprise*."

"The responsibilities of being a parent," Kira said with a smile.

O'Brien looked up. "Yeah, well, Odo should be taking care of his baby right now."

Kira stopped short. She had wanted to help Odo on this mission, but Dr. Bashir had vetoed it. Since she was Bajoran, her immune system was still suffering from carrying a human baby. The doctor insisted that it was too soon after giving birth for her to risk being exposed to tetryon radiation.

Besides, even though she wasn't Kirayoshi's real mother, she didn't like being far away from the baby. She wondered if this bond she felt with him would continue for the rest of her life, or if it would ease with time. She almost hoped the intensity of her maternal feelings would cease. Kirayoshi belonged to the O'Briens, and though he was a part of her life, he was not her son.

She knew Odo felt the same way. The baby changeling hadn't been Odo's child, but that didn't make any difference to Odo. He was risking his life out there in the Badlands to find the thing that had killed his baby.

"I wish we were there too," Kira said.

O'Brien nodded. "The captain will make sure they get the job done."

Kira silently agreed. There was nothing the Emissary couldn't do. In her younger years as a freedom fighter, she had not relied much on religion. But ironically it was her faith in a human, the Emissary, that had brought to life the full power of the Bajoran faith in her.

Kira checked the sensors trained on the wormhole, the Temple of the Prophets, restored to Bajor by the Emissary. The recent discovery of B'hala had finally convinced the last skeptics, including Kai Winn, that Captain Sisko was the Emissary.

The sensor alarm went off, signaling the disruption of subspace in the wormhole.

"The relay has been activated," Kira announced. "Something's coming through the wormhole."

The crew staffing Ops leapt into action. Kira thought it might be a message from the Starfleet vessel, *LaSalle,* in the Gamma Quadrant. But it was early for their daily report.

Kira activated the screen on the main console and entered coordinates for the area where the wormhole would appear. The wormhole spiraled open, brilliant blue and white, emitting verteron particles in millions of streaks of light.

From the very center, where the white shone so

brightly that it lit up DS9, two ships appeared. As the wormhole collapsed again, Kira exclaimed, "Those are Jem'Hadar attack ships!"

"Defensive systems on-line!" O'Brien announced. "Photon torpedoes ready."

Kira listened to the other stations report readiness, while peering closely at the sensor readings. Usually, they didn't see Jem'Hadar attack ships without a larger warship lurking somewhere nearby.

"Lock on photon torpedoes," Kira ordered.

Kira wasn't taking any chances. With DS9's powerful shields and defensive systems, one or two attack ships wouldn't have much of a chance to do any damage. But one of Starfleet's worst-case scenarios included Jem'Hadar attack ships ramming DS9 at several strategic points.

"Attack ships closing," Kira announced.

Her hands were steady as she entered the command to compute their trajectory. A few seconds later, a curving line appeared on the screen, marking the anticipated course of the ships. The line veered close to DS9.

She tracked their course as they reached full impulse power. The reports of the ops crew continued, but most of her attention was on those attack ships. Every second brought them closer to war.

Then the Jem'Hadar ships swept past DS9, staying on course, heading out of Bajoran space. Their trajectory took them in the general direction of Klingon territory.

"Whew!" O'Brien exclaimed. "That was close."

At the edge of the system, the attack ships entered warp and soon disappeared from long-range sensors.

Kira let out her breath. Now she had to report to Captain Sisko. And alert the Klingons to watch out for Jem'Hadar.

Weyoun, the Vorta field supervisor in charge of the Jem'Hadar soldiers, consulted the square sensor window suspended in front of his left eye. When DS9 was long out of sensor range and there were no other vessels in the area, he ordered, "Change course to eight-five-seven mark ninety."

"Changing course," the first announced.

The ship was silent, with no extraneous movements or words from the Jem'Hadar. They were bred for maximum efficiency. Weyoun could sometimes hear the bubble of ketracel-white flowing through the implant tubes in their necks. It was a comfort to know that he held the reigns of so much power.

As the attack ships circled around toward Cardassian space, Weyoun was satisfied, even though it would take several days to reach the Cardassian border. Yet that was preferable to allowing Starfleet knowledge of their ultimate destination.

Now everything was in place. All the Dominion needed was for him to finalize their alliance with the Cardassian Empire, and the invasion of the Alpha Quadrant could begin.

In order to prepare himself for his meeting with Gul Dukat, Weyoun accessed the Dominion receiving station that had been covertly planted in the Alpha Quadrant. It was a passive antenna that roved subspace, recording messages sent by the various superpowers in the region. The unit was hidden within the rocky core of a small meteorite that floated innocuously on the edge of the Bajoran sector.

As he skimmed through the log looking for Cardassian messages, Weyoun noted the most recent acquisition was a transmission sent to DS9 from Captain Sisko on the *Defiant*.

Weyoun had worked with Benjamin Sisko during the first joint Jem'Hadar-Federation mission in the Gamma Quadrant. Together they had prevented renegade Jem'Hadar warriors from controlling an Iconian gateway. Weyoun had praised Sisko's resourcefulness in his report to the Founders.

Weyoun glanced at the edge symbol on his eyepiece. The message included a visual. He replayed the message, and Benjamin Sisko's face appeared on the small view window. With the ease of years of practice, Weyoun ignored the bridge of his ship and focused on Sisko.

He watched the message through once, then replayed it again, stopping at key words to check their meaning. AQS—artificial quantum singularity, a tiny black hole used by the Romulans as a power source in their warbirds. The Jem'Hadar had utterly destroyed the warbirds during the joint Romulan-Cardassian attack on the Founders' world in the Omarion Nebula. No power source had been located.

Weyoun switched screens to view the neighboring sectors. He overlaid their present course on the starfield, noting that it went through a sector adjacent to the Badlands sector. It would only take a minor change in course to investigate this situation.

The diversion would prove risky, since his primary mission was to solidify the Cardassian alliance with the Dominion prior to the invasion of the Alpha Quadrant. Yet Weyoun weighed that against the new threat that would arise from a Federation-Romulan alliance. The success of a Dominion invasion relied on the fact that the empires in the Alpha Quadrant were not allied.

"Change course to three-five-seven mark six-zero," Weyoun ordered.

"Changing course," the first instantly acknowledged.

Weyoun smiled at how easy it was. He had carefully observed Captain Sisko and his Starfleet team during the Iconian gateway mission, as the Founders had ordered. He had noted that everyone in the diverse group of individuals wanted to be informed about everything. That was their weakness. The Dominion was strong because they had the unquestioned loyalty of the Jem'Hadar and the Vorta.

Weyoun sent a brief message to their Cardassian contacts, giving them new coordinates for their meeting place.

It took some time before he got a response. Then Gul Dukat himself hailed them.

The Cardassian's expression was smugly superior, and he spoke as if to a child. *"This is Gul Dukat. I've been expecting you."*

Weyoun instantly distrusted the commander. He had to remind himself that this was the man who would ensure the victory of the Dominion by pledging the support of Cardassia.

"Weyoun," he introduced himself, inclining his head in a gesture of respect. "At your service."

Gul Dukat sounded regretful that he had to correct Weyoun. *"It's not a good idea to meet so close to the plasma storms. There is heavy Federation activity there because of the Maquis. We will meet at the original coordinates."*

Weyoun knew he had been chosen for this mission because of the success of his last one. Many Vorta were finding it difficult to work with the aliens in the Alpha Quadrant. They had become accustomed to obedience in the Gamma Quadrant.

But Weyoun could appreciate a challenge. "There is a situation that requires my attention there."

"What could possibly be more important than our negotiations?" Dukat drawled.

"A Romulan vessel."

Gul Dukat's eyes narrowed, but he clearly did not want to reveal that he wasn't aware of the Romulan ship so close to Cardassian space. *"I don't see what difference that makes."*

"You also don't know that Captain Sisko of the *Defiant* is assisting the Romulan vessel," Weyoun added. "Starfleet and the Romulan Empire—working together again . . ."

Dukat's voice grew harder. *"I see what you mean. That is an unusual situation."*

"I suggest we meet inside the Kamiat Nebula. The emissions will conceal us from their sensors, yet we will be close enough to monitor their transmissions." Dukat hesitated, so Weyoun quickly added, "It wouldn't benefit our cause to have Starfleet and the Romulan Empire form a secret alliance, now would it?"

"Very well," Dukat agreed. *"We will see what Benjamin is up to."*

"In the name of the Founders." Weyoun inclined his head in respect to the Founders, rather than to this Cardassian.

As Gul Dukat signed off, Weyoun leaned against the bulkhead, crossing his arms. He was looking forward to dealing with Dukat and the Cardassians. After this one brief exchange, he was certain the Dominion would be victorious.

Chapter Seven

CENTURION SEYLOK waited for the last repairs to be completed on board the *Bokra*. Though nearly a third of his crew had become ill and were off-duty, the repair team from the *Defiant* had ably assisted their technicians. Seylok had not suffered from the radiation in the slightest, and he believed the crew members who had sickened were simply weak.

Seylok decided that the accident had been a stroke of luck. The Starfleet crew had given him exactly what he needed—additional information about the AQS. Not that Starfleet had admitted they knew it was an artificial quantum singularity. They continued to call it the "Badlands anomaly." But they had provided him with the coordinates of two additional ships that had encountered the object. Combining that information with the data gathered by the Romulan Tal Shiar, Jabak was able to calculate the precise orbit of the AQS.

That's when Seylok had finally informed Sublieutenant Jabak, the quantum specialist, of their true mission. Jabak was the only one allowed inside the locked cargo bay where the equipment was concealed. Jabak had marveled over the advanced graviton field generator that powered a subspace-bubble holding cell for the AQS. The AQS would be directly deposited into the holding cell via a folded space transporter. Once the object was contained, the holding cell would be placed inside the torpedo while they were en route to the wormhole.

"This is the last set of taps," Commander Dax told Seylok. They watched as Rom assisted the senior Romulan engineering technician in removing the last two damaged EPS taps. "The *Bokra* should be ready to power up warp engines after these are replaced."

"Very good," Seylok replied. He didn't add that it was just in time. The AQS would return in its orbit soon. He had hoped to backtrack along the orbit, to set the folded space transporter in place around the edge of the Badlands, out of sensor range of the *Defiant.*

But interfacing the Starfleet-manufactured EPS taps and power circuits with their systems had taken longer than anyone had anticipated.

Dax hit her comm badge. "Ready to receive the last two taps."

"Transporting two electroplasma taps."

Seylok recognized the shape-shifter's gravelly voice. Dax acknowledged, then waited as two large EPS taps materialized in front of her. Seylok bent over to help her pick one up. Together they carried it over to the power conduit and set it down.

Rom and the senior technician were just removing the melted slag of the damaged tap. Seylok and Dax pulled back to give them room to lift the charred mass away.

Seylok had enjoyed conversing with the Trill for the past couple of days. She was an intriguing individual, and unusually attractive for a non-Romulan. It also amused him that the big Klingon was aggressively overprotective of the Trill. Even now, Worf was on the other side of the power conduit, watching them.

For want of anything better to say, Seylok asked Dax in a voice too low to be overheard by Worf, "Aren't you worried about working with a shape-shifter? Giving him access to your most sensitive systems?"

"Odo?" Dax asked. "Odo has proven himself trustworthy many times over."

"I would not be so confident," Seylok said dourly, remembering what had happened to the strike force in the Gamma Quadrant. "Those shape-shifters are born to deceive you. They live to make you believe they are something other than they are."

"Odo's not like that," Dax told him.

Seylok noticed that the Klingon was becoming agitated, so he leaned closer to the Trill. "How can you be so sure? For all you know, *he* could be the shape-shifter." Seylok motioned with his chin toward Worf.

Dax took one look at Worf and laughed, much to the Klingon's discomfort. "Odo isn't that good."

"Maybe he wants you to think he's not proficient," Seylok pressed. "He could be a spy."

Dax laughed even harder. "Not likely. Not after what the Dominion did to him."

Seylok was torn between admiring her and enjoying the barely suppressed fury on the Klingon's face. But Seylok's little game was interrupted by a call from the Starfleet ship. "*Defiant to Commander Worf.*"

Worf stiffened. "Worf here."

"*You are needed on the* Defiant."

As Worf came over to speak to Dax, a small wrinkle of concern appeared between her brows.

"I must return to the *Defiant*," Worf told her, ignoring Seylok.

Dax nodded, and a look of understanding passed between them. Worf held her gaze a few moments too long for military protocol. Then he tapped his comm badge. "One to beam to the *Defiant*."

From that—and from the way the Klingon had stood so close to the Trill—Seylok's suspicions were confirmed. They had an intimate relationship.

As the Klingon dematerialized, Seylok made sure Worf could see him leaning closer to Dax. "Problems?" he asked, wondering why she had chosen that angry, hairy Klingon.

"Odo is sick," she said, still looking worried.

"Oh?" Seylok hadn't known that anything could harm shape-shifters. "From what?"

"The tetryon radiation." Dax briefly shook her head. "It killed a baby changeling Odo found, and now it's made him ill."

Seylok knew this was important information, but his expression never changed. "Some of my crew members are also injured, but your doctor said they could be cured. I'm sure it's the same with your shape-shifter."

"It's more difficult with Odo. Dr. Bashir has to give him regular treatments with an insomatic inductor. That's probably why Worf is needed—to take Odo's station."

Seylok tried to look grave. He was saved from further effort by the Ferengi technician.

"Commander, we're ready to place the new tap," Rom said.

Dax went to help make sure the connections were clean. They had been forced to remove several of the replaced taps and sterilize them, after the diagnostic revealed they'd been contaminated at the junction.

Seylok stayed back; Romulan centurions did not perform manual labor. It gave him a chance to hide his elation. So . . . tetryon radiation was dangerous to shape-shifters. That could be highly valuable information to the Romulan Star Empire.

It also had implications for his current mission. Sublieutenant Jabak had joked about keeping the Dominion busy after the AQS entered the Gamma Quadrant, but Seylok hadn't given it much thought. His goal was to seal the wormhole shut. But if they could target the wormhole on a trajectory that would send the AQS toward the Dominion homeworld, it might wreck more than the shape-shifter's plans to take over the Alpha Quadrant. The entire galaxy could be rid of the menace.

Seylok grabbed a passing technician. "Get Sublieutenant Jabak right away."

"He is off-duty, Centurion," the technician regretfully reported. "He was taken ill with the radiation—"

"I don't care," Seylok said through clenched teeth. He was tired of having his men question his orders. "Have him report to the cargo bay immediately."

"Acknowledged, Centurion," the technician agreed, his eyes wide. The entire crew knew that something important was concealed inside the cargo bay.

Seylok let him go, satisfied. With one last look at Dax as she installed the EPS tap, the centurion headed for the cargo bay. Jabak would arrive and would confirm Seylok's plan to send the AQS through the wormhole to destroy the shape-shifters. Seylok would not settle for anything less. He had waited a long time to prove his worth. On his honor, Romulus was going to get far more than they hoped for with this mission.

The Bashir/changeling managed to get onto the Romulan vessel only once, when he had led a medical team over to assist in treating the Romulans who had been affected by the tetryon radiation. After seeing the centurion's reaction at the sight of Odo, the changeling was particularly careful not to arouse suspicions.

Yet it needed to investigate the situation. The general opinion of the Starfleet crew was that the Romulans were after the AQS. So when the Bashir/changeling found the locked cargo bay, it was unable to resist infiltrating the area.

The changeling waited until it was alone on the deck above, then slipped through the grill that served as a wall. Letting gravity assist it, the changeling quickly dropped onto the deck between the layers of ODN wires and conduits. Unlike Starfleet, the Romulans had not yet learned to seal their internal systems.

Stretching out very thin, it slithered through the deck toward the cargo bay. These walls were formed of many layers, to contain hazardous or precious cargo, but that gave the changeling room to maneuver.

It caressed the door controls, briefly considering opening the door. But the chance of discovery was too great. It found a tiny venting system in the panel and triggered it open. From there it poured into the cargo bay.

It reformed inside the cargo bay as Dr. Bashir. Inside the bay was a complex graviton generator and holding cell—which could certainly contain the AQS. There was also a torpedo shell designed to hold the cell. It only took a moment to determine that the torpedo was programmed to explode the holding cell, releasing the AQS at a predetermined moment.

Obviously the Romulans intended to use the AQS as a weapon.

From the reaction of the centurion against "shape-shifters," the changeling considered it quite possible that the Dominion was a prime target.

The Bashir/changeling shifted its hand into a molecular scalpel with a microfine edge. Working carefully, it partially severed a vital link in the torpedo's navigation system. The navigational array would still perform when tested, but it would only be able to contain the current several more times before the link ruptured, disabling the unit. Then the torpedo would quickly veer off-course.

The entire operation took several minutes. The Romulans and the rest of the medical team hadn't even noticed he was missing. The changeling returned to the deck above, leaving the holding cell and the unusual transportation device alone. It wanted the AQS captured and taken away from the Badlands sector as much as Odo did. The possibility of another changeling being irradiated by the AQS was unthinkable.

All during the next day, the Bashir/changeling waited, wondering if the Romulans would detect his sabotage and raise the alert. But nothing happened. From the messages Seylok exchanged with Sisko, the changeling got the sense that the Romulan centurion was far too confident of success to guard against failure.

So the Bashir/changeling was feeling confident when it returned to the bridge of the *Defiant* with Odo, after Odo's latest treatment. It was not impressed by the way the Starfleet crew had worked nonstop to repair the *Bokra*. Their seeming altruism masked a selfish desire to get the Romulans away from the area so they could capture the AQS. Only the changeling knew that the Romulans were just as intent on trapping the AQS for themselves so they could use its terrible power for destruction.

He should have known the solids couldn't work together for any length of time.

The Bashir/changeling took its seat at the science station to monitor the sensors.

Worf turned from the tactical station. "The away team is requesting permission to return."

"Get them out of there," Captain Sisko ordered. "How much time do we have?"

"Fifty-four minutes," the Bashir/changeling said, following Dax's estimated trajectory of the AQS.

"Not much time," Sisko said thoughtfully.

Dax appeared at the rear of the bridge. "Away team on board, sir. The Romulans are powering up warp drive."

The changeling noticed that Worf glared at Dax as she seated herself. The Klingon had been impatient for her return ever since he had beamed back from the Bokra. The changeling turned away. Jealousy was a solid state of mind, not something it was interested in.

"The Bokra is moving away at half impulse power," Worf reported.

"Proceed to the drop off coordinates," Sisko ordered.

The Bashir/changeling followed the course of the two starships. Both were heading toward the edge of the sensor shadow, but the Defiant planned to stop just inside, where the interference would help conceal what they were doing. The Defiant veered away, but the Bokra seemed to be shadowing them.

Worf saw it as well. "The Bokra is on a parallel course, sir."

Sisko nodded, then Dax reported, "Approaching dropoff coordinates."

"Full stop on the coordinates," Sisko ordered.

"Aye, sir." After a few moments, Dax announced, "Full stop."

The changeling examined the sensor data. The *Bokra* continued on course, increasing to full impulse power. The bridge crew waited impatiently as the minutes ticked by. The changeling could envision the AQS closing on them at warp 9.99.

"*Bokra* at 200,000 kilometers distance." Worf duly reported the progress of the Romulan ship. "Four hundred thousand kilometers distance."

Sisko finally smiled. "Prepare the graviton array for transport to the coordinates."

"Aye, sir," Dax acknowledged. She signaled the science lab below to prepare the graviton trap.

The changeling had observed Dax's efforts to synchronize several standard graviton shield generators in order to produce enough power to trap the AQS. She had used information gleaned from the report made by Geordi La Forge, chief engineer on board the *Starship Enterprise*-D. In 2369, La Forge had successfully extracted the embryos of two quantum-singularity lifeforms from the AQS of a Romulan warbird. Dax and O'Brien had used much of the data in his report to create the AQS trap.

"Graviton array prepared for transport," Dax reported.

"Location of the *Bokra?*" Sisko asked.

"Unknown, sir," Worf said. "They have left our current sensor range. We are still within the sensor shadow of the Badlands."

"Then they can't see us either. Proceed," Sisko ordered.

The changeling noted that the trap materialized far off the port side of the *Defiant*. The array unfurled, expanding in concentric rings to an enormous diameter designed to guide the AQS into its interior. The bulk of the graviton generators created a dark spot in the very center.

"Graviton array activated," Worf reported.

Sisko nodded to Dax. "Take us out of here, Dax."

"Aye, sir." Dax operated the helm with a sure touch, swinging the *Defiant* around the array and retreating. "Full impulse power."

"Impulse?" the Bashir/changeling blurted out. "What about warp?"

"We're still within the sensor shadow," Dax reminded him. "Warp would cause reverberations that could knock the trap off its mark."

"We'll get out in time," Sisko assured him.

The Bashir/changeling wasn't so sure. For a while it looked close, but the changeling carefully ran a simulation of the AQS orbit and range of effects, comparing it against their current trajectory and speed.

"If we continue at full impulse," the Bashir/changeling finally reported. "We will just make it out of range of the most damaging affects of the AQS."

"That's the plan," Sisko said calmly.

"Let's hope our data is correct," the changeling said dourly. "Or we're all going to regret it."

"If you want the full briefing, Julian," Dax said with a grin, "you should get to the bridge on time."

Odo shifted behind the changeling, concerned as

well but too polite to interfere. They had missed the bridge briefing because they were finishing Odo's treatment. The changeling considered Dax's comment to be typical solid behavior, an example of their hasty, hurtful actions.

The changeling felt itself to be the only one braced for the worst—even though they all had proof of the unpredictable power of tetryon radiation.

"Sir!" Worf said. "The *Bokra* has appeared on our sensors. It is returning to the sensor shadow."

The changeling also saw the blip entering the limit of their sensor range.

"Trajectory?" Sisko asked.

Worf reported, "It is on an intercept course with the graviton array. They are at full impulse power."

The changeling quickly calculated the *Bokra* would reach the array long before they could return.

"Open a channel to Centurion Seylok," Sisko ordered.

Worf sent a hail to the *Bokra;* it took precious seconds before the Centurion appeared on the screen.

"Centurion," Sisko said, "Leave the area immediately. The Badlands anomaly is returning and it will disable your ship again."

"We will go in a moment," Seylok assured him. "I just want a closer look at your graviton array."

"We are conducting a scientific experiment. We must ask you to leave the area at once."

Centurion Seylok smiled and reached out one hand. The transmission abruptly ended.

"Damn!" Sisko exclaimed. "What is he up to?"

Susan Wright

"Maybe if we turn back, they'll leave," Dax suggested.

The Bashir/changeling exclaimed, "No!—We can't, sir," he amended, reminding himself of who and what he was. "We would be in danger from the tetryon shockwave. We already have sick crew members on board. I recommend *against* taking the chance of additional exposure."

Sisko gazed at the viewscreen, where the *Bokra* was approaching the graviton array.

"Sir! They are activating their weapons systems," Worf reported.

"Can we get back in time to stop them?" Sisko asked.

Dax grimly shook her head, "No, sir."

"The *Bokra* is targeting the graviton array," Worf announced.

Sisko hit the comm button, sending a message across all bands, "Stop! Centurion Seylok, we are trying to trap the anomaly that damaged your ship!"

The *Bokra* drew closer to the graviton array.

"Firing plasma beam!" Worf reported.

A fine green beam of light was emitted from the lower weapons port of the *Bokra*. It struck the graviton array.

"Direct hit," Worf confirmed.

Two more green beams struck the graviton array, one after another. The lateral rings buckled, starting a chain reaction. Sparks flew from the graviton generators as the array collapsed. The explosion bloomed white and hot orange.

No one needed Worf to confirm that the graviton trap had been destroyed.

Sisko's hand hit the arm of his chair. "Why!? That was completely senseless . . ."

Centurion Seylok appeared on the viewscreen. "Not senseless, Captain Sisko."

The Bashir/changeling realized that the channel was still open from Sisko's attempt to stop the Romulans. The Romulans had heard everything that had happened on the *Defiant*. Devious and fallible solids. . . .

Seylok smiled, his olive skin darkened in a flush of victory. "You don't have to lie anymore, Captain Sisko. We know about the AQS. The *Bokra* was sent here to retrieve it."

Dax felt a sinking in her stomach as she realized that Centurion Seylok was not the hapless, charming captain he'd appeared to be. Even his expression had changed subtly: there was a cynical edge to his smile that hadn't been there before.

Benjamin sounded thoroughly exasperated. "Centurion, why didn't you tell us you were here to get the AQS?"

"Why didn't you?" Seylok retorted sarcastically.

"We only wanted to get that thing out of the Badlands," Sisko told Seylok. "It's a menace."

"Well, it's ours," Seylok said softly. "We will deal with it."

Over his shoulder, Seylok gave an order.

"Sir," Worf said, "An object has appeared approximately 200,000 kilometers away from our original target coordinates. I am having difficulty getting a sensor reading through the shadow."

Seylok never took his eyes off Sisko. "It's a folded-space transporter that will send the AQS directly into a holding cell on board the *Bokra*."

Dr. Bashir said quietly, "Captain, it's in the wrong location. Our estimates of the probable orbit indicates the AQS will miss the transport device."

Sisko turned to Seylok. "Are you sure your calculations are correct, Centurion?"

Seylok lifted one side of his lip. "We are experts on the behavior of quantum singularities. Do not try to tax your minds with such things."

His sardonic smile was the last thing Dax saw as he ended the transmission.

Worf announced, "The *Bokra* is moving away at full impulse power."

"So glad we could be of help," Sisko muttered.

Odo shifted out of the shadow of the bulkhead next to Dr. Bashir, where he had been hiding from Seylok. "I hope the Romulans know what they're doing."

Bashir pointed out, "They won't be able to get out of the danger zone of the shockwave in time. And they're retreating in a direct line from the transporter."

"Then they better hope it works," Sisko commented.

"I'm going to run those orbital calculations again," Dax said thoughtfully.

Sisko nodded. "If they aren't successful, how long will it take for us to construct another graviton array?"

"We have the materials to create two more arrays,"

Dax said. "But it will take nearly twelve hours to assemble one."

"How long until the AQS passes by?" Sisko asked.

"Not long," Dax said. "According to their target location, it could be sooner than we think."

"Are we out of range of the tetryon shock wave?" Sisko asked.

Dr. Bashir hesitated. "Not yet. Since there is a question about the orbital path, I would recommend we erect an additional force field around sickbay to protect the injured from further exposure."

"Do it," Sisko ordered.

Bashir added, "I think Odo should join me in sickbay."

Dax glanced back at Odo. She could tell that the last thing he wanted to do was to leave the bridge at this critical moment in their mission.

"Constable," Bashir said in a warning tone.

"I'm coming, Doctor," Odo reluctantly agreed. He took one last look at the folded-space transporter, so tiny compared to the large array the *Defiant* had deployed.

Sisko must have noticed Odo's concern. "Don't worry, Chief," he assured him. "We'll stop it one way or another."

Dax began preparing the calculation of the AQS orbit, using the Romulan's target point. But she didn't have all the parameters she needed for the orbital simulation.

Dax went over to Worf's tactical station. "Can I get the sensor logs at the time the AQS passed by?"

Worf nodded shortly, accessing the logs. Dax leaned closer, placing her hand on his shoulder. She felt bad, remembering how provoked he had been by Seylok. She had thought at the time that Worf was overreacting. She didn't want him to think he could curtail her interactions with other people.

But now that she knew Seylok had ulterior motives all along, she could see how the centurion had played them against one another. Maybe she shouldn't have continued to talk to Seylok once she saw it bothered Worf so much.

"I'm sorry," Dax whispered, close to his ear.

Worf turned slightly. "You always say that. Yet you do it again."

"I'm a social person," she retorted. "I have to talk to people."

Worf kept his voice low. "You know what I mean, Jadzia. It has been half a year. When will you truly give yourself to me?"

Dax's mouth opened, but there was no light retort she could make. He was serious about this. And he deeply loved her.

"Soon," she whispered.

His eyes widened when he realized what she was saying. Then the barest hint of a smile brightened his face.

Dax felt such love for him that she leaned her brow against his, knowing that he wouldn't allow her to do anything more intimate on the bridge.

With a final squeeze of his shoulder, she returned to the helm. She was truly lucky to have met Worf. Despite their differences, they were perfect for one another. She would give herself to him soon. But she knew her Worf—he would want high drama and romance. And she loved him enough to give him what he wanted.

But she couldn't allow her personal feelings to distract her from the mission at hand. Entering the sensor data along with the information she had gathered from the *Bokra*'s systems—which indicated the *Bokra* had been much closer to the AQS than the *Defiant*—Dax ran the orbital simulation based on the Romulan's target location.

When she saw the results, Dax exclaimed, "We've got trouble. . . ."

"What is it, Old Man?" Sisko demanded.

"The orbital simulation," she said. "I'm putting it on the viewscreen."

The starfield map appeared on the screen. The plasma storms of the Badlands were represented by hundreds of overlapping circles.

"This was where the AQS was first sighted," Dax said as a green dot appeared on the screen. Nearby was a blue dot representing the *Enterprise*. A broken yellow line appeared, tracing the path of the AQS.

"We don't have any contact points for one hundred years," Dax added, "so basically we have to begin again here."

A third dot appeared, then another, and another, as the yellow line connected the various incidents that had been recorded. The yellow line was clearly wobbling in its orbit.

"It's unstable," Sisko said.

"The orbit is decaying," Dax agreed. "If the Romulans are correct, then we only have one, maybe two more orbits before the AQS collides with the Badlands."

"What would happen then?" Sisko asked.

Dax swallowed. "Benjamin, there would be a catastrophic subspace inversion. The subspace distortions would extend well into the nearby sectors and would go on for . . . I don't know how many years. It could disrupt planetary orbital patterns and send tetryon radiation across a vast area of space."

"Bajor," Sisko said.

"We have to stop it." She stared up at the viewscreen, which had returned to the image of the folded-space transporter.

Captain Sisko said, "Let's hope for everyone's sake that Seylok knows what he's doing."

Chapter Eight

EVEN DURING his negotiations with Gul Dukat, Weyoun wore the command headgear with the tiny viewscreen. At first he did it because he was concerned that their meeting place—within the Kamiat Nebula—would be discovered by Starfleet or the Romulans. But the two ships were within the sensor shadow of the plasma storms, and had only limited sensor range.

Nevertheless, Weyoun was himself able to covertly listen in on the messages relayed between the two unsuspecting vessels, mostly uninteresting repair information.

Weyoun continued monitoring the screen because it irritated Gul Dukat. He doled out information to Dukat in selective chunks, carefully noting the Cardassian's reaction.

Dukat was in the middle of discussing the Cardassian terms for an alliance—industrial supplies and assistance in rebuilding the decimated Cardassian fleet—when the image of Captain Sisko appeared on Weyoun's screen. Weyoun immediately held up his hand, cutting off Dukat in midsentence.

"Really!" Gul Dukat exclaimed. "It's not necessary for you to wear that thing *all* the time."

Weyoun ignored the Cardassian, listening as Sisko ordered Centurion Seylok to stand down his weapons. Though Seylok did not respond, the channel remained open. He could hear someone announce, *"Firing plasma beam!"* Then a direct hit was acknowledged. Apparently Starfleet's graviton array had been destroyed.

"Weyoun . . . ," Dukat warned.

"Be silent!" Weyoun demanded. "Something is happening between Starfleet and the Romulans."

"What is it?" Dukat demanded.

Now Weyoun had a visual of the Romulan centurion. His smile was smug, like Dukat's. *"You don't have to lie anymore, Captain Sisko. We know about the AQS. The Bokra was sent here to retrieve it."*

Weyoun told Dukat, "They're fighting over the AQS. The Romulans have destroyed the Starfleet graviton array."

"I don't see how this is relevant to our present negotiations," Dukat said impatiently. *"Obviously* there will be no Romulan-Federation alliance."

But Weyoun knew it was important. In his opinion, Captain Sisko sounded sincere when he said, *"We only wanted to get that thing out of the Badlands. It's a menace."*

Then Centurion Seylok ordered the deployment of the Romuland folded-space transporter. The centurion was typically Romulan as he signed off. *"We are the experts on behavior of quantum singularities. Do not try to tax your minds with such things."*

When the transmission ceased, Weyoun felt disappointed. He had wanted to see more of how Captain Sisko would deal with the situation. Quickly he accessed the data from the long-range probe they had sent to the edge of the sensor shadow around the plasma storms. The Starfleet vessel had withdrawn quite a distance from its previous location. The *Bokra* was also at full impulse power, heading away from the plasma storms.

"I thought we were in the middle of negotiations." Dukat seemed irritated by the lack of a viewscreen. "I'm tired of waiting for you to pay attention."

"The two starships are withdrawing from the plasma storms." Weyoun continued to focus on the readings. "If they come within sensor range, it will alert the Federation that Cardassia is meeting with the Dominion."

"It is unlikely they will come this way," Dukat said dismissively.

"But *if* they do, then it would ruin all our plans," Weyoun retorted. "You must send your warship away. At least if we are discovered, there is nothing to connect us to Cardassia. Your vessel can return for you when our negotiations are completed."

Dukat met his eyes. Neither of them moved for a moment. Weyoun needed to find out how compliant Dukat would be. If the Cardassian was obsessed with the appearance of control, that would make it easier to manipulate him.

But Dukat agreed, "I will send my ship away."

Weyoun bowed his head, standing up and stepping back to give Dukat some privacy to contact his ship. The Cardassian's agreement intrigued Weyoun. Dukat must either be desperate for this alliance—most likely for personal reasons—or he was a supremely confident man. Perhaps both. . . .

Weyoun continued to monitor the two vessels, but neither of them engaged warp drive. Dukat made the appropriate arrangements for his warship to depart the sector.

Weyoun was pleased that the alliance between Starfleet and the Romulans appeared to have been temporary. By simply moving their meeting location, he had gathered important information on the situation in the Alpha Quadrant.

Now, all he needed was for Dukat to cooperate long enough to create an alliance between the Dominion and the Cardassian Empire. Then Weyoun would be able to implement his orders and obey the Founders, assuring the continued superiority of the Dominion in the galaxy.

Odo helped Dr. Bashir erect a level-one medical forcefield around sickbay, which they figured should block any residue of tetryon radiation that managed to penetrate the *Defiant*'s shields.

Several other crewmembers filed into sickbay and were assisted onto cots. They had been sent back to their quarters by Dr. Bashir until ordered to return to the safety of sickbay.

Ensign Teo lay down on the closest biobed. He was one of the unlucky crewmembers who had received nearly 400 rads exposure. As Odo went near the bed, checking the integrity of the forcefield, Teo said weakly, "I can see why your baby changeling got so sick from this thing. It's knocked me flat."

"You know about that?" Odo asked in surprise. He thought only the most senior members of the crew were aware of his personal tragedy.

Teo's good-natured, freckled face was drawn with pain. "Sure, it's why most of us volunteered for this mission. I figured we've got to protect our kids."

Odo was touched. "Thank you. I didn't know. . . ."

"My pleasure," Teo whispered, smiling at the irony of his own words. Obviously this was anything but a pleasant experience.

Odo nodded uncertainly and continued with his work. As long as the forcefield was in place, at least the injured crewmembers wouldn't have to endure additional suffering.

When Odo returned to Dr. Bashir's small office, he asked, "About Ensign Teo . . . he's not permanently damaged, is he?"

"Teo? Oh, he'll recover," Bashir assured him. "His genetic resequencing is proceeding normally. Why?"

Odo focused on the monitor. It showed the folded-space transporter left by the Romulans. "He volunteered for this mission because of what happened to the baby changeling."

"Yes," Bashir agreed. "That's true of most of the crew."

"I thought it was only my friends," Odo said slowly. "I don't even know Ensign Teo. I think we've spoken twice since he was stationed on DS9 . . . I did assist his mate once when he was trying to get their children off a Terillion transport."

"That's probably why he's here," Bashir pointed out. "As security chief on the station, you've had a big impact on these people's lives, Odo. You've probably helped them in ways you don't even remember."

"Perhaps." Odo still felt uncomfortable.

Dr. Bashir gave him an odd look. "You seem surprised that people would want to help you. Perhaps you are more like the Founders than you think you are."

Odo hadn't expected Bashir to hit so close to the truth. "I suppose you're right, Doctor. Did you know that when Quark and I were stranded on that planet a couple of months ago, he called me a misanthrope."

" 'One who hates mankind,' " Bashir said thoughtfully. "Do you hate mankind, Odo?"

"Two months ago, I would have said no," Odo replied. "But now . . . after working more closely with Dr. Mora, I've realized how much I resented his methods of studying me at the Bajoran Institute of Science. His ways were invasive, and I believe, harmful to me."

"Dr. Mora Pol had only the best intentions, I'm sure," Bashir said. "He seemed genuinely concerned about the welfare of the baby changeling."

"Oh, I agree," Odo quickly said. "He looked after

me like . . . a father. But he didn't understand what I was, or how to reach out to me. So . . ."

"So now you don't know how to reach out to people," Bashir finished.

"Yes." Odo continued to watch the static play over the viewscreen, rather than look at Bashir. "But it was worse than that. I realized that deep down inside, I've subconsciously believed that humanoids *are* a danger to my people. In some way, I agreed with their reasoning."

"Because of the way Dr. Mora treated you." Bashir sounded sympathetic. "I wouldn't be surprised if someday you returned to your people, Odo. It's where you belong."

Odo looked at him sharply. Bashir raised both hands in defense, smiling in his boyish way. "Not that we don't want to have you here with us. I'm just thinking of what's best for you. You've never really gotten to know your own people."

"That's true," Odo agreed. "But I can't condone their violent methods. And I no longer believe that humanoids are harmful to changelings. Dr. Mora wanted only the best for me, but I was so selfish I couldn't see that."

"You were a child, Odo," Bashir reminded him. "All children are selfish."

"Well, I've grown up now. And I know there must be a way changelings can live peacefully with humanoids."

"Let's hope so," Bashir said quietly.

Odo was not certain why there was such a flat note

in the doctor's voice. He felt uneasy, wondering if he shouldn't have shared the confidence. But it had been good for him to open up to Mora Pol. Odo had learned a lot about himself, and some of his most primal fears had been set aside. It felt right, and he didn't want to stop now.

"*Estimated ten seconds until the approach of the AQS,*" Sisko announced over the comm.

"Here we go," Bashir said, sitting down in his chair.

Odo kept his eyes on the viewscreen. The folded-space transporter seemed absurdly tiny to stop an object that was super-dense and moving at warp 9.99. The estimated time until impact was counted down on the corner of the screen ... 3 ... 2 ... 1. . . .

For a moment, nothing happened. Then for an instant, the vibration of the advancing shockwave distorted the image, turning the area into a white cloudy patch. The screen exploded in a flash of brilliant light, making Odo flinch. At the same time, he felt the jolt of the *Defiant* as the faster-than-light shockwave hit them.

When the light faded, the folded-space transporter was slowly turning against the star field.

"Wow," Bashir softly exclaimed. "Like stopping a torpedo with one of Captain Sisko's catcher's mitts."

"Did it work?" Odo demanded, examining the area around the transporter. Through the distortion of the sensor shadow, it was difficult to tell if the transporter was still there.

Bashir shrugged slightly as if unsure.

Captain Sisko announced through the comm, "*It ap-*

pears that the Bokra has successfully contained the AQS."

"I wonder if the captain will let the Romulans go?" Bashir asked.

"Why not?" Odo retorted. "As long as that thing isn't endangering anyone, I'm satisfied."

Bashir considered him. "Yes, you should be very happy, Odo. You've achieved your objective."

Odo shook his head. If it was that easy, he just wished someone else had taken the time to stop it a month ago, before it killed the baby changeling.

Chapter Nine

IT WAS the most satisfying moment of Seylok's career: the folded-space transporter had been activated, sending the AQS directly into the holding cell.

Sublieutenant Retal proudly announced, "Containment achieved, Centurion!"

The respect in the sublientenant's manner was deeply gratifying to Seylok. He would always remember Retal's expression after the last of the Starfleet personnel had transported off the *Bokra*. That's when he had finally informed his senior officers that their real mission was to capture the AQS and use it against the Dominion. When the crewmembers realized the import of their mission, it had had an instant effect. Suddenly he was the commander of the most efficient ship in the Romulan Star Empire.

Jabak, the quantum specialist, signaled the bridge

from the cargo bay where the holding cell was set up. *"Containment field holding, Centurion. The subspace bubble has been stabilized."*

"Excellent," Seylok said, letting his pleasure show. "Proceed with the installation in the torpedo."

"Acknowledged, Centurion."

"Plot a course for the Kamiat Nebula," Seylok ordered. "Do we have warp power?"

"Momentarily, Centurion."

They had taken the precaution of powering down the warp engines to avoid burning out the EPS taps again. Seylok had known it was a risk retreating at impulse power, but Jabak calculated that if they retreated in a line with the folded-space transporter, they would escape the brunt of the shockwave.

Of course, if the folded-space transporter had failed, the *Bokra* would have been hit by the AQS. It was a chance Seylok had been willing to take.

"I want warp 4 as soon as you can give it to me," Seylok ordered.

Seylok planned to swing around the Kamiat Nebula, letting it conceal from the *Defiant* their change in course toward the Bajoran sector. He needed to be free of interference to complete the last stage of his mission. They would fire the torpedo at the wormhole from just outside the Bajoran system, and retreat at high warp speed while the AQS did its damage. Jabak had determined the proper entry angle that would ultimately send the AQS toward the Dominion planet.

"En route to the Kamiat Nebula," the helm officer reported.

Sublieutenant Retal cautiously approached the command chair. Now that she saw him as a successful commander, she had gained some proper fear of him. "The damage reports, Centurion."

Seylok scanned the damage reports with a furrowed brow. The *Bokra* had taken a beating on this mission. Their first encounter with the AQS had not been his fault. Despite precautions, there was nothing that could shield them against the singularity when it passed right in front of their bow. Seylok was certain he would not be censured for that—or for allowing the Starfleet team to assist in the repairs. That had ensured the *Bokra* was ready for the next approach of the AQS.

But the delay in planting the folded-space transporter had taken its toll. They had been hit by the remnants of the tetryon shock wave. Almost a third of the new EPS taps had overloaded. But since warp drive had been off-line prior to impact, they could restore low warp power soon. Shields were down to 60 percent.

Yet Seylok knew that Tomalok would approve his tactic of destroying the *Defiant*'s graviton array. It had not been strictly necessary, since Starfleet had placed it in the wrong location. But Seylok knew it would send a clear signal to the *Defiant* not to interfere when he took possession of the AQS. And it had worked.

Seylok kept his narrowed eyes on the *Defiant*'s trajectory inside the sensor shadow. They were on an intercept course with the folded-space transporter. The *Bokra* went into warp long before they reached it, but Seylok didn't need sensors to know that the Starfleet ship would pick up the folded-space transporter. They were also probably scanning the area where the AQS had been captured, to make a full report of their failure to Starfleet Headquarters.

Seylok ordered his crew to push the EPS taps and maintain warp 4 as they traveled through the sector. He also ordered them to continue with long-range scans to be sure that the *Defiant* didn't try to catch up to them and challenge them for the AQS.

When the *Bokra* finally neared the edge of the Badlands sector, Seylok began to relax. The difficult part was completed. He would be hailed as a hero when they returned to the Romulan Star Empire. He would get his choice of assignments—perhaps even in the Praetor's administration.

Seylok was preparing to leave the bridge for the cargo bay to inspect the installation of the holding cell. But Sublieutenant Retal announced, "Centurion, we're reading unusual energy signatures coming from the Kamiat Nebula."

"On screen," he ordered.

The twisted ion clouds appeared on the screen. The blue-white opaque clouds were lit by bright blue flares along the outermost edges, where energy discharged into normal space.

As the *Bokra* approached the nebula, Seylok examined the readings. "That doesn't look like a natural energy source."

"Affirmative," the sublieutenant replied. "It must be a starship. A large vessel, to judge by the angle of the energy output."

The computer ran a comparison for energy signatures. Seylok almost ordered the helm to veer off, but when he saw the results, his hands clenched on the arms of the command chair. "Jem'Hadar!"

"They will ambush us!" Sublieutenant Retal exclaimed.

"Evasive maneuvers," Seylok snapped. "Take us into the nebula."

The nebula emissions would disguise their exact location within the nebula; there they could elude the Jem'Hadar. It was probably not what the Jem'Hadar had expected—concealed inside the nebula, waiting to attack at the last possible moment, giving the *Bokra* no chance of escape. It was a typical Dominion tactic, and it had destroyed the Cardassian-Romulan joint strike force.

"Entering the nebula," the sublieutenant announced.

Seylok remembered how the Tal Shiar had died by Jem'Hadar treachery. "Now we shall see who survives."

"Control over the Maquis colonies must revert to Cardassia," Dukat was saying. "It is our right—"

Weyoun held up one hand, interrupting Dukat. "The *Bokra* is changing course. It is entering the Kamiat Nebula."

Dukat leaned forward, his pose of detachment shattered. "Have they detected our ships?"

Weyoun abruptly stood up and left the small conference room, returning to the bridge. He did not object when Dukat and his aide followed.

"Engage engines," Weyoun ordered the first. "Take us to coordinates six-six-one mark ten."

Weyoun intended to stay within the nebula, while avoiding the Romulan vessel.

The first implemented Weyoun's orders. "Vessel still closing."

Weyoun ordered, "Evasive maneuvers."

Dukat grabbed Weyoun's shoulder. "Get away from them before it's too late!"

Weyoun twisted away from Dukat. He spoke very slowly. "Don't . . . ever . . . touch me."

Dukat was glaring, obviously wishing he were in control of the ship. But faced with Weyoun's unwavering blue eyes, Dukat raised his hands slightly, signaling that he would back down.

"As long as you know what you're doing," Dukat warned.

Weyoun told the first, "Prepare to attack."

The *Bokra* shuddered as they entered the ion clouds of the nebula. Seylok noted that the energy discharge strained the integrity of their shields.

"Search pattern Beta," Seylok ordered.

He would not allow the Jem'Hadar to destroy this mission. But he couldn't forget all the Tal Shiar who had failed against the Jem'Hadar.

"Centurion!" the sublieutenant exclaimed. "We have two Jem'Hadar attack ships within visual range."

"Target their weapons systems," Seylok ordered. "And fire!"

The *Bokra* swerved to avoid enemy fire while sending plasma beams at both Jem'Hadar attack ships.

"Direct hits!" the sublieutenant exclaimed.

Their sensor readings were distorted by the effects of the nebula, but Seylok could tell from the visual that the heavy shielding on the attack ships had deflected the plasma beams.

"The Jem'Hadar are retreating," the sublieutenant reported.

Seylok wanted to order the *Bokra* to retreat, but he couldn't allow the Jem'Hadar to take the offensive. "Come around for another attack," Seylok ordered.

The crew's clear admiration and confidence in his ability reassured him. They would prevail.

"Target weapons," the sublieutenant ordered.

Seylok gave the command, "Fire!"

As the *Bokra* passed, the two Jem'Hadar vessels suddenly veered apart. Still, the plasma beams struck both heavily shielded attack ships.

The Jem'Hadar began to speak as one. "I am dead. As of this moment we are all dead. We go into battle to reclaim our lives. This we do gladly because we are Jem'Hadar. Remember, victory is life."

Weyoun ordered, "Attack pattern R-three-seven."

Dukat was looking around at the heretofore silent Jem'Hadar. "You can't attack! The *Defiant* could be in sensor range."

Weyoun briefly considered ordering Dukat off the bridge. But during their negotiations, the Cardassian had been far too demanding for a people whose empire had been invaded and destroyed by the Klingons. He needed a lesson in Dominion resolve. Weyoun decided

that he would make an example of the Romulans, purely for Dukat's benefit.

Weyoun nodded to the first, who passed on the attack pattern to the other Jem'Hadar ship.

"No one defies the Dominion and survives," Weyoun
said softly.

The Bokra's evasive maneuver brought them face to
face with one of the Jem'Hadar ships, which fired con-
tinuously as they passed. Seylok could see the *Bokra*'s
shield rates dropping to 50 percent, then 40 percent.

"Take us out of the nebula!" he ordered.

They would be invisible to the attack ships for just a
moment as they passed through the energy discharge.
As the flashing blue barrier grew closer, Seylok stead-
ied himself for a rough ride, since their shield integrity
was low.

"Prepare the Defor maneuver," Seylok told the sublieutenant. Retal quickly gave the orders.

The *Bokra* hit the energy-discharge barrier, and there
was a sense of sliding out of control as they left the
nebula. But it was only the shield harmonics vibrating
the ship.

Seylok held on. "Execute Defor!"

The centurion braced himself as the *Bokra* entered
the Defor maneuver, named for a legendary Romulan
captain of the century-long Romulan-Vulcan war. Engaged in Defor, the *Bokra* sank rapidly along the edge
of the nebula, hugging the energy discharge to mask its
passage.

It had worked well against the Vulcans because it

was not logical to subject a starship to the energy discharge of a nebula when the shields were already strained by battle.

Seylok intended to duck back into the nebula as soon as the Jem'Hadar emerged: they could pass directly through the nebula and warp away from the other side, before the Jem'Hadar had located them again.

Suddenly, the sublieutenant announced, "Jem'Hadar!"

Simultaneously, the Jem'Hadar ships punched through the energy barrier, one on either side of the *Bokra*.

Seylok stood up. "Take us into the nebula!"

Weyoun allowed himself to smile at Dukat. "They attempted the Defor maneuver. Now we are positioned on either side of the *Bokra*, in perfect formation to attack."

Dukat narrowed his eyes. "How did you know what maneuver they would execute?"

Weyoun motioned to the first, who gave the order to fire. As the hum of phased polaron beams filled the bridge, Weyoun told Dukat, "The Dominion knows everything."

Chapter Ten

THE BASHIR/CHANGELING was helping Odo disengage the forcefield around sickbay when the *Defiant* finally stopped its subtle shuddering. For days the changeling had been trying to ignore the irritating vibrations caused by the sensor shadow. It sighed in relief, imitating the solids.

"We're out now," Odo said.

The Bashir/changeling activated his screen again. "I wonder where the Romulans are. Oh, there. . . ."

Odo came up next to it to see. The *Bokra* was slightly fuzzy from the distance, as it passed the Kamiat Nebula. Suddenly, the *Bokra* changed course and dived into the nebula.

"What are they doing?" the changeling exclaimed.

"I don't know, but it looks very strange," Odo commented. They waited a few minutes, but nothing happened. "I'm going to the bridge to find out."

Odo had turned away when the Bashir/changeling exclaimed, "The *Bokra* is out of the nebula again!"

The Romulan ship slipped along the edge of the nebula, partially concealed by the deep-blue energy discharge. "What are they doing?" Odo wondered aloud, returning to its side.

The Bashir/changeling didn't understand much of the solids' behavior. But the way the *Bokra* had abruptly dived into the nebula and then re-emerged, only to subject itself to the high-level discharge, was truly incomprehensible.

"We've gone to warp 7," the changeling noted. "I bet Captain Sisko is going after the *Bokra*—"

"Look!" Odo exclaimed, pointing to one side of the tiny image of the *Bokra*. "Another starship."

The Bashir/changeling felt a thrill of recognition. "That's a Jem'Hadar attack ship."

"And there's another one," Odo agreed. "They have the *Bokra* surrounded."

The Bashir/changeling looked with longing at the two Jem'Hadar ships. Their phased polaron beams shot out again and again, pounding the Romulan vessel. The changeling was pleased that the Dominion had somehow known about the danger posed by the Romulan possession of the AQS. Not that it needed this display of omniscience to make it quite confident that the impending invasion of the Alpha Quadrant would succeed. Nothing could stop the Founders from securing both quadrants and ensuring their continued prosperity.

On the viewscreen, two more beams of phased polarons—and the aft section of the *Bokra* exploded.

"There she goes!" the Bashir/changeling exclaimed.

The *Bokra* hung against the nebula for a brief moment, a jagged hole where the aft section had once been. Then a blinding white light voided the screen, even brighter than the one that had accompanied the transport of the AQS into the Romulan holding cell.

The Bashir/changeling remembered to throw its arms up as if protecting its sensitive solid eye nerves. But it continued to watch the radiation monitors on the medical console. The tetryon count didn't rise. The *Defiant* was far enough away that the shockwave hadn't reached them.

Odo was staring at the screen "The AQS! It's been released."

"The *Defiant* was far enough away not to be affected," the Bashir/changeling told him.

"I've got to get to the bridge," Odo insisted.

Since the worst had already occurred, the Bashir/changeling left sickbay in the hands of its assistants and followed Odo to the bridge. It needed to know what had happened to the two Jem'Hadar ships. They were so close—yet it was impossible for it to contact its own people.

The crew were just getting sensors back on line as the changeling entered the bridge. Worf was reporting, "The Jem'Hadar ships have been disabled by the AQS. Both appear to be withdrawing into the Kamiat Nebula."

The changeling quickly took over the science station to confirm Worf's readings. One Jem'Hadar ship slipped into the nebula before the changeling could get a sensor lock. The other limped along much more slowly. The Bashir/changeling read the presence of twenty Jem'Hadar soldiers, one Vorta, and two Cardassians on board.

It instantly realized that this was information that Starfleet must not see. It could damage the success of the invasion. The Bashir/changeling wiped the short-term sensor log, preventing the bioreadings from being sent to the computer banks for permanent storage. The changeling replaced the empty segment of the log with a loop of the sensor information from the first vessel, the one it didn't have a chance to get a lock on.

The second Jem'Hadar ship slipped into the nebula.

The Bashir/changeling held its breath; but Worf had been too busy scanning for weapons signatures to check for life-signs.

"I'm reading life-signs," the changeling reported. "I can't tell if their life-support is intact."

"Do we go after them?" Dax asked.

Captain Sisko stood up, looking at the blue-and-white nebula. "No, they took their chances when they attacked the *Bokra*."

The Bashir/changeling felt contempt for the solids. Of course they would leave the Jem'Hadar in danger. It was their cavalier attitude toward life that made them so dangerous. It proved once again the need for the Dominion to control the solids. If left on their own they would destroy themselves and everyone else. Even though the Bashir/changeling knew it personally would not survive the invasion, it was glad to give its own life for the highest cause that existed—peace in the galaxy.

"Where is the AQS?" Sisko asked.

Worf was working. "The AQS entered the nebula and emerged from the other side. According to its current trajectory, it is entering Federation territory."

Sisko heard the sudden hush among the bridge crew. After watching their fellow shipmates sicken from the tetryon radiation despite the special shielding, they knew what sort of damage the AQS could do if it passed close to any population centers.

"I want to know exactly where that AQS is heading," Sisko ordered.

"We have the coordinates of the *Bokra* when it exploded," Dax said. "And we have the exact point of exit from the nebula. Using the Romulan orbital simulation, we should be able to pinpoint its trajectory."

"Meanwhile, follow the AQS," Sisko ordered. "Warp 9."

"Sir, that is in violation of Starfleet protocol," Worf reminded him.

"I know that, Mister Worf," Sisko replied. "I'm sure in this case Starfleet Headquarters would agree."

Dax acknowledged, inputting the coordinates in the helm. Then she handed the helm over to her relief and took over the science station from Dr. Bashir.

The doctor willingly relinquished his seat. "We were lucky this time to be so far away."

"Lucky!" Sisko repeated in disbelief. They had failed in their mission, and now there was an even bigger mess to clean up. Sisko still couldn't understand why the Jem'Hadar had attacked the *Bokra*.

"Benjamin, I have the trajectory," Dax informed him.

"On screen," Sisko ordered.

The outer segment of the spiral arm of the Milky Way appeared on the viewscreen. Federation territory encompassed vast distances in space: it would take nearly ten years to cross it at warp 8.

Sisko noted the Cardassian border at the top, and at the bottom the border of the Klingon Empire. A thick sprinkling of stars curved down the center of the screen.

"This is the Badlands," Dax explained, as a pinpoint red dot began to blink. "The AQS is moving faster than the speed of light, so it's way ahead of us now."

A dotted yellow line slashed across the upper portion of Federation territory. The *Defiant* appeared much further back.

Sisko began to relax. "It's leaving Federation territory."

"So it appears," Dax said grimly. "But look what happens when the simulation continues."

The AQS proceeded directly up, heading for the empty space between the arms of the galaxy. But when it reached the edge where the stars were more sparsely scattered, it abruptly turned at a 45 degree angle.

"What happened?" Sisko's eyes widened as the yellow line cut through the stars. "It's going towards the most densely populated section of the Federation!"

Dax magnified the area where the AQS had swerved

off course. "That flashing light is the Great Pulsar, a rotating neutron star. The magnetic field will catch the AQS long enough to distort its trajectory. Unfortunately, the gravitational forces aren't as strong as the Badlands plasma storms, so the AQS won't enter orbit."

The yellow dotted line continued to mark the AQS's passage, as it cut a swath through the Federation and entered the Klingon Empire. Worf made a rumbling noise deep in his throat as he watched the AQS slice into his people's territory.

"We can't catch up to it, Captain. But if we cut across *here*," Dax indicated with a red line, "and proceed at maximum warp, we could intercept it after it swings around the Great Pulsar."

"How fast?" Sisko asked.

"Warp 9.8," Dax replied. "For the next seven hours."

Sisko rubbed his hand against his mouth. "Will the engines hold up?"

Dax shrugged one shoulder, while Worf stoutly insisted, "The *Defiant* is a strong ship. She can do it."

"We have no choice but to try," Sisko agreed. "Lay in the course, helm." He turned to Dax. "Do you have time to construct another graviton array?"

Dax slowly shook her head. "I don't see how we can do it that fast."

"Then we'll have to use the folded-space transporter the Romulans so kindly left behind."

Dax's eyes widened. "I haven't even looked at it, Benjamin. I'm not sure we can operate it."

"You have seven hours, Old Man," Sisko retorted.

Dax opened her mouth to protest, but he added, "I *know* you can do it."

"All right," Dax said. "But I'll need Rom's help."

"Take whomever you need," Sisko agreed. "Just get me that trap by the time we reach the coordinates."

Dax immediately left. Sisko waited until the bridge was calm before ordering Worf, "Prepare a secured subspace message to be sent to Starfleet Command."

Worf acknowledged, preparing the message to be sent. "You may record, sir."

Sisko straightened up. This had to be done—and done quickly. "This is Captain Benjamin Sisko of the Starship *Defiant*. The AQS was captured and accidentally released again when the Romulan scout ship, *Bokra, w*as destroyed by two Jem'Hadar attack ships. The AQS is heading toward Federation territory. We are attempting to intercept. We recommend you evacuate the systems in the path of the AQS."

Sisko closed the message, wondering if that terse statement adequately conveyed his resentment toward the Dominion.

"Send the secured message along with the logs of the AQS trajectory and our planned interception. Also send them the logs of the Jem'Hadar ambush," Sisko ordered. He sat back and stared at the starfield while Worf complied.

Now they had to trap the AQS.

But Sisko found himself thinking more about the Jem'Hadar than the AQS. He had an eerie double vision, as if the attack on the *Bokra* was playing over and over again, a series of catastrophic Jem'Hadar battles. Watching them destroy the Romulan ship had prompted an image that he couldn't shake: hundreds of Jem'Hadar ships streaming through the wormhole. Vast convoys of Dominion supplies and weapons. All aimed at the Alpha Quadrant.

Chapter Eleven

ODO ASSISTED DAX and Rom in examining the Romulan folded-space transporter. Actually, Odo fetched mug after mug of raktajino for Dax, and also offered his shape-shifting abilities, forming tools helpful in manipulating the unusual fittings.

He was bent over, one arm elongated and shaped to fit a ring-like attachment, while Rom worked under him adjusting the trajector of the transporter. They needed to be able to hold the device in position when the displacement wave of the AQS struck it. A normal tractor beam wouldn't work with the folded-space technology, since it incorporated subspace matrixes.

Odo stifled a groan, knowing the impulse was a holdover from his recent solid days. He knew how badly it would have hurt his back to stand like this.

Now, it was more a matter of irritation, having to keep so still.

But he didn't say anything. He felt guilty about the damage the AQS was causing even as they worked on a way to stop it.

"Almost got it," Rom said cheerfully.

"Remember to put the coupling on before you tighten it," Dax warned.

Odo knew that he wasn't responsible for the destruction being wrought on Federation systems. His plan to trap the AQS had resulted in the *Defiant* being in the area to assist the Romulans repair their ship. They had done everything they could.

But Odo felt guilty because it was the Founders who controlled the Jem'Hadar, and they had attacked the *Bokra* and loosed the AQS on the Federation. His fellow changelings bred the Jem'Hadar purely for battle. And they had genetically altered them in such a way that they lacked the vital isogenic enzyme ketracel-white; and they controlled the Jem'Hadar's access to the white, through the Vorta . . . What kind of despicable, ruthless people would do that?

Odo knew. It was the same people who had sent their babies to distant points of the galaxy, forcing them to find their way home. Odo had felt a deep sense of betrayal ever since the Founders told him that he had been expendable, a test case to see how kind the solids were in the Alpha Quadrant.

Odo knew that Captain Sisko was concerned about their future. He also knew that the Founders would make another move against the Alpha Quadrant, that this time it could be an all-out invasion. He agreed with the captain that they had to be prepared.

"That's it!" Rom announced. "You can let go now, Odo."

Odo withdrew his arm, standing back to give Dax room to check the results. "Looks good," she said. "We should be able to hold the transporter in place like the *Bokra* did."

"How close will we have to be?"

"Too close," Dax replied. "We'll do what they did—retreat in a direct line from the transporter. Most of the shockwave dissipates to the sides and behind the AQS because it's moving so fast."

"Doesn't that mean the AQS will hit us if it misses the transporter?" Rom asked, worried.

"I guess that means we can't miss," Dax retorted. "Help me get it on the transporter pad."

Odo helped attach the antigrav pallets to move the folded-space transporter onto the *Defiant*'s transporter pad. They would beam it to the coordinates, then hold it in place with a tractor beam keyed to the correct trajector sequence.

The folded-space transporter was small, but it controlled a great deal of power through its use of antineutrinos. The Romulans apparently made it a habit to employ powerful devices like their AQS warp engines and the folded-space transporter. Odo preferred the Federation's decision to find alternative and safer means of performing the same task. But in this case, surely it would take a Romulan device to stop a Romulan singularity.

Rom stayed behind to make last minute adjustments, but Odo followed Dax back to the bridge. She reported to Captain Sisko, "The folded-space transporter is ready."

"Just in time," Sisko pointed out.

Dax took her usual seat at the helm. "Approaching the target coordinates."

"We only get one chance at this," Sisko reminded them all. "Are you sure the coordinates are correct?"

Worf turned from the tactical station. "I have run the simulation through the best Starfleet programs with all of the available data. The Great Pulsar has been studied and its gravitational rates are precisely calibrated. There is a 91 percent accuracy rate."

"We've had worse odds," Sisko murmured.

Odo knew there were planets in the path of the AQS. He hoped they wouldn't miss, or millions would be killed. People were already dying from exposure to the tetryons, and one of the planets it had passed reported that their environmental ecosystems had been permanently affected by the radiation.

"Dropping out of warp speed," Dax announced.

Odo could feel the shudder run through the ship as the powerful warp drive finally ceased. It had been a strain on the *Defiant* to come so far so fast. It was probably the only Starfleet vessel able to perform such a feat.

"Take warp drive off-line," Sisko ordered.

"Powering down engines," Dax confirmed. "Plasma venting from all electroplasma taps."

"How long before the AQS arrives?" Sisko asked.

"We have enough time to beam the transporter to the coordinates," Dax reported, "and retreat at full impulse power to 400,000 kilometers."

Worf added, "We must stay within that range to hold the transporter in place. I have enhanced the shields to protect the crew from tetryon radiation."

Odo stepped closer to Captain Sisko's chair. "Sir, we have the transporter, but we don't have a holding cell to put the AQS in. Where will we transport it?"

"I've done some research on folded-space technology," Sisko replied. "It provides instantaneous transport across great distances. We'll send it light-years from here, and place it outside of our galaxy."

Dax glanced over her shoulder. "It would take millions of years for it to cross empty space. It would probably never hit another galaxy. That's perfect, Benjamin."

"I thought so." Sisko had a satisfied smile on his face. "But we have to get it right the first time. Make sure Rom gets the correct transport coordinates."

Worf acknowledged, working on the problem. "Sending transport coordinates."

After a few moments, Rom's uncertain voice came over the comm. "Coordinates set. Shall I read them back?"

Everyone said yes at the same time, making Dax laugh. Rom slowly read back the coordinates as Sisko and Worf cross-checked.

"That looks like it," Sisko said. "Transport the folded-space transporter to the target area."

"Transporting," Worf announced.

On screen, the tiny device twinkled against the darkness. It looked even smaller than before, making Odo think how odd it was that it could have such a big impact on galactic events. But it could save millions of lives. . . .

"Folded-space transporter in place," Worf confirmed. "Tractor beam holding."

"Retreat at full impulse," Sisko ordered.

Odo hoped all their hard work would pay off. If the trajector lock failed, then the transporter would be buffeted out of position by the tetryon shockwave. If the coordinates were off—even slightly—the AQS would miss it completely.

The *Defiant* retreated at full impulse power, keeping a remote hold on the folded-space transporter. Odo took a seat at the secondary science station to watch. There were more messages coming in from the star systems that were unfortunate enough to have been in the path of the AQS. Emergency calls for help were being sent out from over a dozen vessels. But that was only a tiny fraction of the devastation that would be wrought by the AQS if it wasn't stopped here.

Sisko glanced over at Odo. "Shouldn't you be in sickbay?"

"My morphogenic matrix has been stabilized," Odo said. He would rather stay on the bridge and take his chances along with the rest of the crew. Dr. Bashir had told him to come down to sickbay, but Odo had ignored the order. It didn't feel right hiding in safety while everyone else was at risk.

"Estimated ten seconds until the approach of the AQS," Sisko announced to the entire ship.

Odo noticed that Dax glanced at Worf, and the two exchanged a long look. It must feel good to have that sort of bond with another being.

"Get ready, people," Sisko said, bracing himself in his chair.

Odo kept his eyes on the sensor monitor. Readings indicated the folded-space transporter hung in the far distance. The time until impact was counted down on the corner of the screen . . . 3 . . . 2 . . . 1 . . .

At that instant, the stars seemed to shift, and Odo felt an odd dislocation, as if the galaxy itself had rocked from the impact. Odo was watching the sensors rather than the screen, so when the white flash of light occurred, he could see it as a wave of nearly pure tetryon neutrinos. In a microsecond it was gone.

Gravity cut out, and the *Defiant* dropped away under him. Odo drifted up into the air, losing some of his solid definition. While the others let out involuntary exclamations, Odo wasn't bothered by the sensation. He shot out a tentacle to magnify sensors to check on the folded-space transporter.

The transporter device was slowly turning against the star field, exactly like the first time.

Gravity quickly reengaged, depositing everyone roughly to the floor. Odo gracefully resettled in his chair. He activated the long-range sensor probe they had planted in the projected path of the AQS, but it detected no unusual levels of tetryon radiation. The AQS was gone.

"It worked," Odo said quietly.

The others were pulling themselves back to their stations.

Sounding out of breath, Dax reported, "The transporter was activated. The AQS is now ten thousand light-years away."

"Confirmed," Worf agreed. "The energy dispersal rate from the transporter is consistent with the first entrapment."

Odo relaxed back in his seat, another holdover from his solid days. It was done. There would be no more baby changelings killed by the AQS. It would damage no more ships and kill no more people.

"That's one problem out of the way," Sisko said quietly.

Odo agreed. Now all they had to deal with was the Dominion.

"Let's go home," Sisko ordered. "We've got a lot of work to do."

Inside the Kamiat Nebula, Weyoun gave the last orders for the Jem'Hadar to repair their vessel. Several of the Jem'Hadar had sickened and quickly died from the tetryon radiation. But Weyoun and Dukat had received only low doses of radiation. Weyoun considered that to be a sign of good fortune from the gods.

Weyoun planned to transfer to Gul Dukat's Cardassian warship when it arrived, so they could complete their negotiations while his own attack ships were repaired. Dukat was excessively pleased at this, which gave Weyoun new hope that he would be able to manipulate the Cardassians through their pride.

Because of the damage to his attack ships, Weyoun would not be able to return to the Gamma Quadrant for at least another few days, delaying the inevitable. Yet Weyoun was not unduly distressed. As far as he was concerned, the invasion of the Alpha Quadrant had already begun.

OUR FIRST SERIAL NOVEL!

Presenting, one chapter per month . . .

The very beginning of the Starfleet
Adventure . . .

STAR TREK®
STARFLEET: YEAR ONE

A Novel in Twelve Parts

by
Michael Jan Friedman

Chapter Five

Daniel Hagedorn yawned and stretched. Then he pushed his wheeled chair back from his monitor and the blue-and-gold ship schematics displayed on it.

True, the captain and his colleagues had submitted their recommendations regarding the *Daedalus* earlier in the day. But that didn't mean their responsibility to Director Abute was fully discharged—at least not from Hagedorn's point of view.

He meant to come up with further recommendations. A whole slew of them, in fact. By the time he set foot on the bridge of the *Daedalus* or one of her sister ships, he would know he had done everything he could to make that vessel a dead-sure success.

Abruptly, a red message box appeared against the blue-and-gold background. It was from Abute, advising each of his six captains that they would begin interviewing prospective officers the following day.

Hagedorn nodded. He had been wondering when the process would get underway.

There were to be a few rules, however. For instance,

Abute wanted each vessel to reflect the variety of species represented in the Federation, so no captain could bring aboard more than a hundred human crewmen.

Also, Hagedorn couldn't draw on established military officers for more than half his command team. Clearly, the director wanted both the defense and research camps represented on each vessel's bridge.

The captain grunted. They could keep their *Christopher* crews intact after all, but only if some of their officers were willing to accept a demotion. Clearly, practicality would be taking a backseat to politics in this new Starfleet—not that he was surprised, given the other developments he had seen up to that point.

On the other hand, no one would be foisted on him— neither alien nor Earthman. That was one point on which Hagedorn wouldn't have given in, even if Abute had handed the *Daedalus* to him on a silver platter.

After all, the lives of the captain and his crew might one day depend on a particular ensign or junior-grade lieutenant. He wanted that individual to be someone who had earned his way aboard, not a down payment in some interplanetary quid pro quo.

With a tap of his keyboard, Hagedorn acknowledged receipt of the director's message. Then he stored the *Daedalus*'s schematics and accessed the list of officer candidates Abute had compiled.

Frowning, the captain began to set up an efficient interview schedule. He promised himself that by noon the following day he would know every bridge officer under his command.

Cobaryn was relaxing in his quarters, reading Rigelian triple-metered verse from an electronic book, when he heard the sound of chimes.

It took him a moment to remember what it meant—that there was someone in the corridor outside who wished to see him. Getting up from his chair, the captain crossed the room and pressed a pad on the bulkhead. A moment later, the doors slid apart.

Cobaryn was surprised to see Connor Dane standing there. "Can I help you?" the Rigelian asked.

The Cochrane jockey frowned. "You drink?" he asked.

Cobaryn looked at him. "You mean . . . do I partake of alcoholic beverages? In a public house?"

Dane's frown deepened. "Do you?"

"In fact," the Rigelian replied, "I do. That is to say, I have. But why are you inquiring about—?"

The human held up a hand for silence. "Don't ask, all right? Not where we're going, or why—or anything. Just put the damned book down and let's get a move on."

Cobaryn's curiosity had been piqued. How could he decline? "All right," he said. Then he put the book down on the nearest table, straightened his clothing, and accompanied Dane to their mysterious destination.

Dane tossed back a shot of tequila, felt the ensuing rush of warmth, and plunked his glass down on the bar.

The Afterburner's bartender, a man with a bulbous nose and a thick brush of gray hair, noticed the gesture. "Another?" he growled.

"Another," Dane confirmed.

He turned to Cobaryn, who was sitting on a stool alongside him. The Rigelian was nursing a nut-flavored liqueur and studying the human with his bright red eyes. They were asking a question.

"I know," said Dane, scowling. "You still don't understand why I asked you to come along."

Cobaryn smiled sympathetically. "I confess I don't."

"Especially since I never said a word to you the whole way from Rigel to Earth Base Fourteen."

"That does compound my curiosity, yes," the Rigelian admitted. "And even after our battle with the Romulans—"

"I sat in the bar by myself," Dane said, finishing Cobaryn's thought.

He watched the bartender replace his empty shot glass with a full one. Picking it up, he gazed into its pale-green depths.

"Why do I need company all of a sudden?" the human asked himself. "Because I'm out of my element here, that's why." He looked around the Afterburner. "Because I have no business trying to be a starfleet captain."

The Rigelian shrugged. "From where I stand, it seems you would make an excellent captain. You have demonstrated intelligence, determination, the courage to speak your mind. . . ."

"You mean at that meeting this morning?" Dane dismissed the notion with a wave of his hand. "That wasn't courage, pal. That was me losing my patience. I got hacked off at the idea of a bunch of lab coats telling me what I could and couldn't have."

"Nonetheless," Cobaryn insisted, "you said what no one else would have thought to say. You saw a danger to your crew and you did not hold back. Is that not one of the qualities one should look for in a captain?"

The human chuckled humorlessly. "Anyone can open a big mouth. You don't have to be captain material to do that."

"Perhaps not," the Rigelian conceded. His mouth pulled up the corners. "But it does not hurt."

Dane hadn't expected Cobaryn to make a joke. He found himself smiling back at his companion. "No," he had to allow, "I guess it doesn't."

Cobaryn's grin faded a little. "And what about me?"

The human looked at him askance. "What *about* you?"

"I am hardly the obvious choice for a captaincy in Starfleet. The only vaguely heroic action I ever undertook was to ram my ship into that Romulan back at Earth Base Fourteen—and that was only after I had determined with a high degree of certainty that I could beam away in time to save myself."

Dane was starting to feel the effects of the tequila. "Listen," he said, leaning closer to the Rigelian, "they didn't pick you for your courage, Cobaryn. They may have picked you for a whole lot of reasons, but believe me . . . courage wasn't one of them."

The Rigelian looked at him thoughtfully. "You are referring to my ability to command a vessel in deep space?"

"Maybe that's part of it," the human conceded, "but not all of it. Just think for a second, all right? This United Federation of Planets they're building . . . it's not just about Earth. Technically, we humans are only supposed to be a small part of the picture."

"A small part . . . yes," said Cobaryn. His bony, silver brow furrowed a bit. "That is why Director Abute imposed a quota on the number of humans who can serve under us."

Dane pointed at him. "Exactly. And if they're encouraging us to include nonhumans in our crews and command staffs. . . ."

For the first time, the Rigelian actually frowned in his presence. "You are saying I was picked to be a captain because I am an alien?"

"Hey," said Dane, "you're better than that. You're an alien who's demonstrated that he can work alongside humans—who's demonstrated that he actually *likes* to work alongside humans. Do you have any idea how many people fit that particular description?"

"Only a few, I imagine."

"A few?" The Earthman sat back on his stool. "You may be the only one in the whole galaxy! To the mooks who are engineering the Federation and its Starfleet, you're as good as having another human in the center seat—which is what they'd *really* like."

Cobaryn weighed the comment. "So I am a concession

to the nonhuman species in the Federation? A token appointment, so they will not feel they have been ignored in the selection process?"

"Hey," said Dane, "it seems pretty clear to *me*. But maybe that's just the cynic in me talking."

The Rigelian didn't say anything for a while, though the muscles writhed in his ridged temples. Finally, he turned to his companion again. "I take it a human would resent the situation as you have described it?"

"Most would," Dane confirmed.

A knot of silver flesh gathered at the bridge of Cobaryn's nose. "And yet," he said, "I find I do *not* resent it. After all, Earth's pilots clearly have more tactical experience than the pilots of any other world. And if a nonhuman is to work with them, why not choose one who has already shown himself capable of doing so?"

Dane drummed his fingertips on the mahogany surface of the bar. "You can find the bright side of anything, can't you?"

"So I have been told," the Rigelian conceded.

The human shook his head. "Pretty amazing."

Cobaryn smiled at him again—or rather, did his best impression of a smile. "Amazing for a human, yes. But as you will recall, I am a Rigelian. Among my people, everyone looks on the bright side."

Dane rolled his eyes. "Remind me not to stop at any drinking establishments on your planet."

The Rigelian looked as if he were about to tender a response to the human's comment. But before he could do that, someone bellowed a curse at the other end of the bar.

In Dane's experience, people bellowed curses all the time, almost always for reasons that didn't concern him. Unimpressed, he threw back his tequila and felt it soak into him. But before long he heard another bellow.

This time, it seemed to come from a lot closer.

Turning his head, the Cochrane jockey saw a big, balding fellow in black-and-gold Earth Command togs headed his way. And judging by the ugly, pop-eyed expression on the man's face, he was looking for trouble.

"You!" he said, pointing a big, blunt finger directly at Dane. "And you!" he growled, turning the same finger on Cobaryn. "Who do you think you are to imitate space captains?"

"I beg your pardon?" said the Rigelian, his tone flawlessly polite.

"You heard me!" roared the big man, pushing his way through the crowd to get even closer. "It's because of you two butterfly catchers that I wasn't picked to command a Starfleet vessel!"

Cobaryn looked at Dane, his face a question. "Butterfly catchers?"

Keeping an eye on their antagonist, who was obviously more than a little drunk, the Cochrane jockey made a sound of derision. "It's what Stiles and the other military types call us."

Call you, he corrected himself inwardly. He had never had an urge to do a stitch of research in his life.

"Well?" the balding man blared at them. "Nothing to say to Big Andre? Or are you just too scared to pipe up?"

By then, he was almost within arm's reach of his targets. Seeing that there would be no easy way out of this, Dane got up from his seat and met "Big Andre" halfway.

"Ah," grated the balding man, his eyes popping out even further. "So the butterfly catcher has some guts after all!"

"Actually," said Dane, "I was going to ask you if I could buy you a drink. A big guy like you must get awful thirsty."

Big Andre looked at him for a moment, his brow furrowing down the middle. Then he reached out with lightning speed and grabbed the Cochrane jockey by the front of his uniform shirt.

"I don't need any of your charity," the big man snarled, his breath stinking of liquor as he drew Dane's face closer to his. "You think you can take away what is mine and buy a lousy drink to make up for it?" He lifted his fist and the smaller man's shirt tightened uncomfortably. "Is that what you think, butterfly catcher?"

Dane had had enough. Grabbing his antagonist's wrist, he dug his fingers into the spaces between the bones and the tendons and twisted.

With a cry of pain and rage, Big Andre released him and pulled his wrist back. Then the expression on his meaty face turned positively murderous. "You want to fight me? All right—we'll fight!"

"No," said Cobaryn, positioning himself between Dane and the balding man. "That will not be necessary." He glanced meaningfully at his companion. "Captain Dane and I were about to leave . . . were we not?"

"I don't think so," said a sandy-haired civilian, who was half a head shorter than Big Andre but just as broad. "You'll leave when Captain Beschta gives you permission to leave."

"That's right," said a man with a thick, dark mustache, also dressed in civilian garb. "And I didn't hear him give you permission."

Dane saw that there were three other men standing behind them, all of them glowering at the Starfleet captains. Obviously, more of Big Andre's friends. Six against three, the Cochrane jockey mused. Not exactly the best odds in the world—and as far as he knew, the Rigelian might be useless in a fight.

"You want to leave?" the big man asked of Cobaryn, his expression more twisted with hatred than ever. "You can leave, all right—when they carry you out of here!"

And with remarkable quickness, he launched his massive, knob-knuckled fist at the Rigelian's face.

Dane couldn't help wincing. Big Andre looked big and strong enough to crack every bone in the Rigelian's open, trusting countenance.

But to Dane's surprise, Big Andre's blow never landed. Moving his head to one side, Cobaryn eluded it—and sent his antagonist stumbling into the press of patrons that had gathered around them.

Big Andre roared in anger and came at the Rigelian a second time. Dane tried to intervene, tried to keep his new-found friend from getting hurt, but he found himself pulled back by a swarm of strong arms.

Fortunately for Cobaryn, he was able to duck Big Andre's second attack almost as neatly as he had the first. Again, the human went hurtling into an unbroken wall of customers.

But Big Andre's friends were showing up in droves and pushing their way toward the altercation. Some of them, like Big Andre himself, wore the black and gold of Earth Command. Others were clearly civilians. But they all had one trait in common—a rabid desire to see Dane and the Rigelian pounded into something resembling pulp.

"Surround them!" one man called out.

"Don't let 'em get away!" barked another.

Dane tried to wriggle free of his captors. But before he could make any headway, he felt someone's boot explode in his belly. It knocked the wind out of him, forcing him to draw in great, moaning gulps of air.

Then he felt it a second time. And a third.

When his vision cleared, he could see Big Andre advancing on Cobaryn all over again. The man's hands were balled into hammerlike fists, his nostrils flaring like an angry bull's.

"I'll make you sorry you ever heard of Starfleet!" Big Andre thundered.

"That's enough!" called a voice, cutting through the buzz of the crowd the way a laser might cut an unshielded hull.

Everyone turned—Dane, Cobaryn, the big man and everybody else in the place. And what they saw was the commanding figure of Dan Hagedorn, flanked by Hiro Matsura and Jake Stiles.

Hagedorn eyed his former wingmate. "Leave it alone," he told Beschta.

The big man turned to him, his eyes sunken and red-rimmed with too much alcohol. "Hagedorn?" he snapped.

"It's me," the captain confirmed. "And I'm asking you to stop this before someone gets hurt."

Beschta laughed a cruel laugh. "Did they not hurt *me?*" he groaned, pointing at Dane and Cobaryn with a big accusing finger. "Did they not take what should rightfully have been mine?"

"Damned right!" roared a civilian whom Hagedorn had never seen before in his life.

A handful of other men cheered the sentiment. The captain had never seen them before either. Apparently, Beschta had picked up a few new friends in the last couple of weeks.

If the big man had been the only problem facing him, Hagedorn would have felt confident enough handling it on his own. But if he was going to have to confront an unknown number of adversaries, he wanted to make sure he had some help—and to that end, he glanced at his companions.

First he looked at Stiles, who knew exactly what was being asked of him. But Stiles shook his head from side to side. "This isn't any of our business," he said in a low voice.

"Like hell it isn't," Hagedorn returned. Then he turned the other way and regarded Matsura.

The younger man seemed to waver for a moment. Then his eyes met Stiles's and he shook his head as well. "I can't fight Beschta," he whispered, though he didn't seem entirely proud of his choice.

Hagedorn nodded, less than pleased with his comrades' responses but forced to accept them. "All right, then. I'll do this myself."

Turning sideways to make his way through the crowd, the captain tried to get between Beschta and his intended victim. But some of Beschta's new friends didn't like the idea.

"Where do you think you're going?" asked one of them, a swarthy man with a thick neck and broad shoulders.

Hagedorn didn't answer the question. Instead, he drove the heel of his hand into the man's nose, breaking it. Then, as the man recoiled from the attack, blood reddening his face, the captain collapsed him with a closed-handed blow to the gut.

If anyone else had had intentions of standing in Hagedorn's way, the incident changed their mind. Little by little, Hagedorn approached Beschta, who didn't look like he was in any mood to be reasoned with.

"Don't come near me!" the big man rumbled.

The captain kept coming. "That's not what you said when I saved your hide at Aldebaran."

"I'm warning you!" Beschta snarled, his eyes wide with fury.

"You won't hit me," Hagedorn told him with something less than complete confidence. "You can't. It would be like hitting yourself."

"Stay away!" the big man bellowed at him, his voice trembling with anger and pain.

"No," said the captain. "I won't."

For an uncomfortable fraction of a second, he thought Beschta was going to take a swing at him after all. He tensed inside, ready for anything. Then his former comrade made a sound of disgust.

"I thought you were my friend," Beschta spat.

"I am," Hagedorn assured him.

"They turned me away," the big man complained. "The bastards rejected me. *Me*, Andre Beschta."

"They were wrong," said the captain. "They were stupid. But don't take it out on these . . . " With an effort, he kept himself from using the term *butterfly catchers,* " . . . gentlemen."

Beschta scowled at Cobaryn and Dane, who was still in the grip of some of his allies. "You're lucky," he said. "Had Captain Hagedorn not come along, you would have been stains on the floor."

The Cochrane jockey had the good sense not to answer. Hagedorn was happy about that, at least.

The big man indicated Dane with a lift of his chin. "Let him go. He's not worth our sweat."

The men holding Dane hestitated for a moment. Then they thrust him toward Hagedorn. The Cochrane jockey stumbled for a step or two, but caught himself before anyone else had to catch him.

Off to the side, Beschta's friends were picking up the man Hagedorn had leveled. He looked like he needed medical attention—though that wasn't the captain's concern.

"Come on," he told Dane and Cobaryn. "Let's get out of here."

As they headed for the exit, the Rigelian turned to Hagedorn. "Thank you," he said with obvious sincerity.

"You're welcome," Hagedorn replied.

As he left the place, he shot a look back over his shoulder at Stiles and Matsura. They were guiding the hulking Beschta to a table, taking care of their old wingmate.

A part of Hagedorn wished he could have done the same.

Hiro Matsura felt more torn over what he had seen than he cared to admit. In the heat of the moment, he had taken the side of one trusted colleague over another. And on reflection, he wasn't at all sure that he had settled on the right decision.

Soberly, he watched Hagedorn and the two butterfly

catchers leave the Afterburner. Then he negotiated a course to the bar.

"What'll it be?" asked the bartender.

"Brazilian coffee," said Matsura. "Black."

The bartender smiled. "For Beschta?"

Matsura nodded. Obviously, his friend had made a name for himself. "Sorry about the brawl."

The bartender dismissed the apology with a gesture and went to pour out some coffee. "It's okay," he said. "We haven't had a good knock-down-drag-out in weeks." Then he laid a hot, steaming mug on the wooden bar.

Picking up the coffee, Matsura paid the bartender and made his way back to Beschta's table. Stiles had pulled out a chair opposite the big man and was trying to calm him down.

"Listen," the captain was saying, "how long do you think those butterfly catchers are going to last? A month, Andre? Two, maybe? And when they're gone, who do you think they're going to call for a replacement?"

Beschta shook his head stubbornly. "Don't patronize me, Aaron. I may be drunk, but I'm not an imbecile. I have no chance. Zero."

"Here," said Matsura, placing the mug of coffee in front of the big man. "This will make you feel better."

Beschta glared at him for a moment, bristling with the same kind of indignation he had shown earlier. Then, unexpectedly, a tired smile spread across his face. "Some example I'm setting for you, eh, Hiro?"

Matsura didn't know what to say to that. A couple of days ago, he had still thought of himself as Beschta's protégé. Now, he was beginning to feel that he might be more than that. "Drink your coffee," was all he could come up with.

The big man nodded judiciously. "That's a good idea. I'll drink my coffee. Then I'll go home and sleep for a week or two."

"Now you're talking," said Stiles.

Seeing that Beschta was all right for the moment, he clapped him on his broad back and went over to Matsura. "Hagedorn was out of line," he said in a low voice.

"You think so?" asked the younger man.

Stiles looked at him with narrow-eyed suspicion. "Don't *you?*"

Matsura folded his arms across his chest. "The more I think about it, the more I wonder. I mean, Dane and Cobaryn could have gotten hurt. What would that have proved?"

Stiles looked like a man who was trying his best to exercise patience. "Listen," he said, "I didn't want to see people injured any more than you. But this is war, Hiro, and those two butterfly catchers are the enemy."

Matsura considered his colleague's position. "If it's a war, I'll do my best to help win it. You know that. But standing there while Dane and Cobaryn needed our help . . . it was just wrong."

His colleague considered him for a while longer. "You know," he said at last, "I disagree with you a hundred percent. If I had to do it over again, I'd do exactly the same thing."

Matsura started to protest, but Stiles held up a hand to show that he wasn't finished yet.

"Nonetheless," the older man continued. "this is no time for us to be arguing. We've got to be on the same page if we're going to get the kind of fleet we're aiming for."

Stiles was right about that, Matsura told himself—even if he was wrong about everything else. "Acknowledged."

His colleague smiled a little. "Come on. Let's get Beschta home."

Matsura agreed that that would be a good idea.

Look for STAR TREK Fiction from Pocket Books

Star Trek: The Next Generation®

Encounter at Farpoint • David Gerrold
Unification • Jeri Taylor
Relics • Michael Jan Friedman
Descent • Diane Carey
All Good Things • Michael Jan Friedman
Star Trek: Klingon • Dean W. Smith & Kristine K. Rusch
Star Trek VII: Generations • J. M. Dillard
Metamorphosis • Jean Lorrah
Vendetta • Peter David
Reunion • Michael Jan Friedman
Imzadi • Peter David
The Devil's Heart • Carmen Carter
Dark Mirror • Diane Duane
Q-Squared • Peter David
Crossover • Michael Jan Friedman
Kahless • Michael Jan Friedman
Star Trek: First Contact • J. M. Dillard
Star Trek: Insurrection • Diane Carey
The Best and the Brightest • Susan Wright
Planet X • Michael Jan Friedman
Ship of the Line • Diane Carey
Imzadi II • Peter David

#1 *Ghost Ship* • Diane Carey
#2 *The Peacekeepers* • Gene DeWeese
#3 *The Children of Hamlin* • Carmen Carter
#4 *Survivors* • Jean Lorrah
#5 *Strike Zone* • Peter David
#6 *Power Hungry* • Howard Weinstein
#7 *Masks* • John Vornholt
#8 *The Captains' Honor* • David and Daniel Dvorkin
#9 *A Call to Darkness* • Michael Jan Friedman
#10 *A Rock and a Hard Place* • Peter David
#11 *Gulliver's Fugitives* • Keith Sharee
#12 *Doomsday World* • David, Carter, Friedman & Greenberg
#13 *The Eyes of the Beholders* • A. C. Crispin
#14 *Exiles* • Howard Weinstein
#15 *Fortune's Light* • Michael Jan Friedman
#16 *Contamination* • John Vornholt
#17 *Boogeymen* • Mel Gilden

Star Trek: Deep Space Nine®

Star Trek®: Day of Honor

Book One: *Ancient Blood* • Diane Carey
Book Two: *Armageddon Sky* • L. A. Graf
Book Three: *Her Klingon Soul* • Michael Jan Friedman
Book Four: *Treaty's Law* • Dean W. Smith & Kristine K. Rusch
The Television Episode • Michael Jan Friedman

Star Trek®: The Captain's Table

Book One: *War Dragons* • L. A. Graf
Book Two: *Dujonian's Hoard* • Michael Jan Friedman
Book Three: *The Mist* • Dean W. Smith & Kristine K. Rusch
Book Four: *Fire Ship* • Diane Carey
Book Five: *Once Burned* • Peter David
Book Six: *Where Sea Meets Sky* • Jerry Oltion

Star Trek®: The Dominion War

Book 1: *Behind Enemy Lines* • John Vornholt
Book 2: *Call to Arms . . .* • Diane Carey
Book 3: *Tunnel Through the Stars* • John Vornholt
Book 4: *. . . Sacrifice of Angels* • Diane Carey

Star Trek®: The Badlands

Book One: Susan Wright
Book Two: Susan Wright

Star Trek: *Strange New Worlds* • Edited by Dean Wesley Smith
Star Trek: *Strange New Worlds II* • Edited by Dean Wesley Smith